ABDUCTED

ABDUCTED

ROBERT SWARTWOOD

RMS Press

ISBN-13: 978-0692676219
ISBN-10: 069267621X

www.robertswartwood.com

For Brian Keene—
Tour Guide to the Underworld

ABDUCTED

1

It was just past three o'clock in the morning when Ashley Gilmore pulled into the gas station.

A bell jangled when she opened the door of the station's minimart, causing the clerk behind the counter—a young guy with long hair and beard, maybe twenty-three years old—to glance her way before doing a double take.

"Hi," he said, smiling as he sprang up from the stool he'd been sitting on. "How's it going?"

Ashley smiled at him but said nothing as she wandered down the first aisle, out of his line of sight. A TV on the counter played the news, or what sounded like the news. It was simply background noise as she moved from one aisle to the next, her hand hovering over the display of snacks, their wrappers a bright iridescence, before settling on a tiny bag of pretzels. Next she detoured by the drinks and selected a large bottle of water. As she let the door slam shut, she saw a sign on the cooler announcing a sale of two bottles for three dollars, but she didn't bite.

At the counter, the clerk hadn't sat back down. He smiled at her as she approached.

"Forgot to tell you," he said. His nametag read SETH. "Happy Thanksgiving."

She forced another smile. "Happy Thanksgiving to you too."

"Did you have a nice holiday?" He squinted at her scrub bottoms. "Oh shit, you had to work, didn't you?"

Smiling again, she nodded.

"You're over at the hospital?"

Another nod.

"So you missed out on a big Thanksgiving dinner?" He sounded genuinely bummed at the mere notion of this.

"There's always leftovers."

Seth shook his head sadly. "Still, that sucks. I feel your pain. I've been working a double. No turkey dinner for me. I did try some of the turkey jerky we have over in aisle three, but it tasted like shit."

She nodded, her gaze momentarily shifting toward the TV. It was playing CNN, a pretty reporter talking to the camera while a picture of two men hung over her right shoulder. Mug shots. Both looked scruffy with long hair; one had a beard, the other had a goatee.

Seth said, "Crazy, huh?"

"What's that?"

His eyes went wide. "The jailbreak!"

She glanced back at the TV. "I heard a little bit about it. When did it happen?"

"Yesterday morning. At least, that's when they found the two convicts had escaped. They dug right out of their cell, just like in that Morgan Freeman movie." He nodded at the TV. "That's them right there. The one on the left is Neal Palmer. The other is Sean Wescott. They were both in for murder."

"Murder?"

"Yeah, the guy on the right, Wescott, they say he murdered an FBI agent a couple years ago. The other guy, Palmer, murdered someone too, but, I mean, shit, an *FBI* agent? That's hardcore."

"Where'd they escape from?"

His eyes, incredibly, went even wider. "Wrightsville. It's only, like, forty miles away from here." He paused, considering something, and shifted on one foot so he could look past her out the front windows. "Where are you parked?"

Ashley said nothing, keeping her focus on the TV.

"I'm not trying to be creepy or anything," he said, "it's just that those two assholes could be anywhere."

Ashley motioned at the tiny bag of pretzels and bottle of water. "Can I ..."

"Sure, sure." Seth nodded quickly as he started scanning the items. He paused, squinted over at the cold cases. "You know, there's a special on this water. Two for three."

"I just want one bottle," Ashley said.

"But, like, you're saving a dollar. You're practically getting the other bottle for free."

On the TV, they'd cut to another reporter, this one a man, stationed outside the prison. He stood bundled in a jacket, a microphone to his mouth. He said, "I'm here in Wrightsville, New York, standing outside the Wrightsville Correctional Facility where sometime last night two inmates managed to escape."

Ashley said, "I'm okay with just the one bottle."

Seth shook his head as if this made no sense. "But—"

"Look"—her voice taking on a hard edge—"I appreciate the thought, but it's been a long night. I just worked a double shift. My feet are killing me. I'm exhausted. All I want to do is get home to my kid and sleep ten hours."

For an instant, the hurt flashed in Seth's eyes. But he blinked it away, nodded, said, "I totally understand. Hell, I can't wait until I get home. Gonna play some *Fallout* and then sleep for, like, *twelve* hours. Anyway, that will be three forty-seven."

She handed him a crumpled five-dollar bill.

As he made change, he asked her if she'd like a bag.

"No thanks," she said, already collecting her items and turning toward the door.

Seth said, "Would you, um, like me to walk you to your car?"

She turned back around as she reached the door, forcing another smile. "Thanks, but I'll be okay."

She opened the door—that bell jangling again—and stepped out into the frigid night.

The highway was deserted except for one pair of headlights in the distance. She watched them as she walked toward the Mazda parked around the corner.

A state police car slowed almost to a stop as it drove past the gas station, not pulling in. The trooper glanced at her, at the minimart, then at the bank across the highway, before the car's engine revved as it accelerated away.

Ashley stepped off the sidewalk. The Mazda was only yards away. The tiny bag of pretzels and bottle of water clamped in one hand, she used her other hand to dig into her jacket pocket for the keys. As she brought them out, a man stepped toward her, materializing from the shadows by the building.

Ashley gasped, dropping the pretzels and water, and held up her keys as if they presented some kind of protection.

The man took another step toward her and then stopped.

For a moment, there was complete silence.

Which allowed her to hear the crunch of pavement behind her as another man stepped up close and pressed the tip of a knife against her neck.

"Scream"—the new man's breath hot on her ear—"and I'll cut your throat."

2

Ashley didn't scream. She barely made a sound. Her body went rigid as she stared ahead at the man standing in front of her.

He looked to be in his late-thirties, tall, black thick-framed glasses. He wore jeans and workman boots and a jacket. He took another step toward her. Reached out and grabbed the keys in her hand.

She didn't let go.

The man behind her said, "Let go of the fucking keys."

She loosened her grip just enough for the keys to drop from her hand.

The man in front of her caught the keys in midair.

Ashley found her voice, a stunted tremulous whisper. "Please don't hurt me."

The blade pricked her skin as the man behind her said, "Shut up."

The man now with the keys tested the driver's side door. She hadn't locked it. He slipped in.

Keeping the tip of the knife against her throat, the man behind her opened the back door. "Get in."

She was sobbing now. "No, please, don't."

"*Get in.*"

She didn't move.

He grabbed her arm and yanked her to the back of the car. He pushed her into the backseat, started to climb in after her when a voice outside the car spoke.

"What the fuck?"

Seth stood on the sidewalk, a cigarette in one hand, a lighter in the other. Ashley could see him from where she was in the backseat. The shock in his eyes as he realized what was happening. He turned at once, started running back toward the minimart entrance.

The man in the driver's seat was out of the car in an instant. He disappeared from view. A second or two went by and then they reappeared, both of them, the man dragging Seth around the corner into the shadows.

The man with the knife still had the back door open. He said to her, "Don't do anything stupid," and stepped out of the car, slammed the door shut.

Even with the doors closed and the windows up, she could hear their voices.

The man holding Seth said, "What should we do with him?"

The man with the knife scanned the parking lot as if the answer would be evident. Finally, he shrugged. "Doesn't look like we have a choice."

He plunged the knife into Seth's stomach.

Ashley screamed.

She didn't see what happened next, already turning in her seat, fumbling with the handle, and pushing open the door. A copse of trees stood directly behind the gas station. She sprinted for it. Halfway there, the man with the knife caught up with her. He grabbed for her arm but she managed to slip out of his grip. When he went to grab her arm again, she wasn't so lucky. He yanked her to a halt and spun her around and pressed his face to hers, his angry breath rank from cigarettes.

"What the fuck did I tell you?"

Her eyes darted down to the knife in his hand, its blade dripping blood. "Please," she sobbed, "please don't do this."

He shoved her forward toward the Mazda. The other man stood over Seth, who lay on the ground, his hands on his stomach.

Seth was still alive. Groaning in pain, yes, but still alive.

The man with the knife shoved her into the car. He ducked his head down, growled, "Do that again and you're dead," and slammed the door shut.

Ashley watched him storm around the car to where the other man stood with Seth on the ground.

The other man said, "You *stabbed* him?"

The man with the knife didn't say anything. He stared at Seth for a couple seconds, then leaned down and ran the blade across Seth's throat.

Ashley screamed again.

The other man said, his voice flat, "What the fuck?"

The man with the knife searched Seth's pockets. He stood back up with a ring of keys, motioned at a Saturn parked behind the building.

"Drag him over to the car."

The other man said, "You *killed* him."

"Drag him over to the fucking car," the man with the knife growled, already headed in that direction.

He shuffled through the keys until he found the one that belonged to the Saturn and popped the trunk and waited while the other man dragged Seth's dead body to the car. The man set the knife aside and grabbed Seth's feet and together the men shoved Seth into the cramped trunk, and then the man slammed the trunk shut and grabbed the knife and started back toward the Mazda. Back toward her.

Ashley continued to sob.

The other man said, "Now what?"

The man with the knife watched her from outside the car.

He said, "Hurry inside. Turn off the lights. Turn off the power. Destroy the surveillance system if you can find it. Take what you can from the register."

The other man glanced at Ashley in the car. "Don't kill her too."

The man with the knife said, "I won't. Just hurry!"

The other man hurried away.

The man with the knife slowly approached the Mazda, watching her. He held the knife at his side, its blade still dripping blood.

He didn't get inside. He waited. A minute passed. The lights at the pumps first flickered, then dimmed, then went out entirely. So did the lights in the minimart. The other man appeared a few seconds later. He carried what looked like a hard drive.

The man with the knife said, "What's that?"

"The surveillance system." The man opened the driver's door and slid back in, tossing the hard drive down in the passenger-side footwell. He closed the door, inserted the key in the ignition, but paused.

The man with the knife got into the backseat beside her. He smelled of sweat and body odor. He said, "What's wrong?"

The other man said, "There's a baby bottle up here." He glanced back at her. "You have a baby?"

She nodded, still sobbing. "Yes. Yes, I do. Please don't—don't hurt me."

The other man looked at his partner. "She has a baby."

"Who fucking cares?" said the man with the knife. "Get us the fuck out of here."

The other man glowered at his partner for a long moment. Then he turned back to the wheel, adjusted his glasses, started the engine, and reversed them out of the shadows.

3

Henry Barnes—the warden at Wrightsville Correctional Facility—sat in his office in the dark. He leaned back in his chair, his eyes closed, trying to sleep. But he couldn't sleep. Not after what had happened today. Or was it yesterday already?

His cell phone vibrated on his desk.

He opened his eyes, leaned forward, glanced at the screen.

A text from his wife.

I LUV U :-)

Henry picked up the phone. He started to type back a reply but instead pressed the button to call her.

Claire said, "Hey."

"You're still up?"

"I couldn't sleep. I've just been sitting here watching CNN. They keep replaying the press conference."

"How did I look?"

A smile in her voice. "Handsome."

Henry stared into the dark of his office but said nothing.

"It'll be okay," Claire said.

"It will not be okay."

"This wasn't your fault."

"I'm the warden, Claire. Everything that happens here is my fault."

"They'll catch these guys."

"Even if they do, somebody will need to be held responsible. Who do you think that somebody is going to be?"

This time, Claire said nothing.

"How are Aidan and Melissa?"

"They're worried. They stayed up with me past midnight but both have gone to bed."

"Did you guys end up eating the turkey?"

"We did, but it wasn't the feast I'd planned. There are a lot of leftovers. You'll be eating turkey sandwiches for the next month."

"I'm glad Aidan and Melissa were able to come home for the holiday. Melissa's graduated, has a job, she's fine. Aidan's got one more year of college, but if anything should happen we have enough in savings to help pay his tuition until he graduates."

"Henry, stop."

"No, Claire, we have to be honest with ourselves about this. I didn't want to have this conversation with you yet, but we might as well get it out in the open. They're going to force me into early retirement if they don't outright fire me. That means we could lose the pension. Claire, I don't know what we'll do if we lose the pension."

She was quiet for a couple seconds, the cellular line connecting them humming quietly.

"It will be okay."

Henry opened his mouth, started to speak, but shook his head.

Claire said, "Can't you come home for a bit, try to get some sleep?"

"I shouldn't. Not until we know at least something."

"Those men couldn't have just disappeared."

"It depends on when they escaped. They could have a five-hour head start."

Another silence. Henry could hear the TV through the phone, the quiet sound of two pundits discussing what a major screw-up this had become.

Claire said, "I love you."

"I know. I love you too."

"It will be okay."

Henry closed his eyes, shook his head, but before he could speak there was a knock at the door.

"Claire, I need to go. I'll call you later."

He disconnected just as the door opened, and Lewis Riddell, his Correctional Captain, poked his head in.

Lewis was a tall, muscular black man. The light in the corridor shined off his bald head.

"Henry, you okay?"

"What is it, Lewis?"

"Why are the lights off?"

"Do you have something for me?"

"I do." Lewis stepped into the room. "Mind if I turn on the lights?"

"Be my guest."

Lewis flicked on the overhead fluorescents and marched over to stand directly in front of Henry's desk.

"Tell me you have something good," Henry said.

"That depends. I just spoke to Janice down in Nursing. She told me about Maryann Webster."

"Who?"

"She worked here as a part-time nurse. Was here just over a year."

"And?"

"Janice said she had frequent contact with Neal Palmer."

"How much contact?"

"Not a lot—just nine contacts in the last year—but it's more than any of the other nursing staff. Apparently a couple months back Palmer complained of stomach pains which allowed him to see the nurse several times."

"What about Wescott?"

Lewis shook his head. "Sean Wescott almost never went to Nursing."

"Lewis, am I to assume the idea here is that Maryann Webster is somehow involved in the escape?"

"That's the thing, sir. We don't know for sure."

"Have you spoken to her?"

"No."

"Why not?"

"She put in her two-weeks."

"When?"

Lewis said, "Her last day was yesterday."

4

Janice in Nursing couldn't tell them much. She said that Maryann Webster had been quiet but a good worker. She got along well with the staff and the prisoners.

"Lewis tells me Maryann saw Neal Palmer nine times."

Janice nodded, glancing past Henry at Lewis standing in the doorway of the nursing station. "That's right. At least, that's how many times are recorded on the computer."

"Do you think there could have been other visits?"

"Based on how complete Maryann kept her paperwork? I highly doubt it. She was very professional. There's no way she would—" Janice paused, frowning now at Henry. Her voice lowered to a conspiratorial tone. "Do you think she has something to do with this?"

"At this point," Henry said, "I don't know what to think. All we know for sure is at 5:30 yesterday morning guards found Neal Palmer and Sean Wescott missing from their cell. That they had escaped through a goddamned hole in the wall, excuse my language."

"But Maryann"—Janice made a face like she had just bit into

a lemon—"no, I can't imagine Maryann had anything to do with this."

"You understand why I'm asking you, though, right?"

Janice allowed a short nod.

"So please," Henry said, "can you think of anything about Maryann that seemed ... *off* to you?"

Janice took a moment to think about it. Her eyes narrowed slightly when she whispered, "I think she may have been a Democrat."

Henry noted the MCCAIN/PALIN 2008 campaign button still hanging off the corkboard above Janice's computer.

"Anything else?" he said.

She took another moment, her eyes still narrowed, and then shook her head. "Nothing else that comes to mind. To be honest, she was an excellent worker. I even offered her full-time hours a couple months back, but she turned it down."

"Did she say why?"

"If she did, I can't remember."

"What about a significant other?"

Again Janice shook his head. "No husband that I'm aware of. Never heard her mention a boyfriend either."

"Is there anything you can tell us about her personal life?"

This time, Janice didn't answer. She just shrugged.

Henry glanced back at Lewis, irritated. He asked Janice, "Would there be anybody who would know? Anybody she was close to?"

"Like I told you, she kept to herself. She was an excellent worker, but she didn't talk much. I wish I could tell you more."

Henry thanked Janice for her time and started to turn away.

Janice asked, "Do you really think Maryann helped those two?"

Henry turned back to force a smile. "Right now, we don't know what to think. Based on what you've told me, I can't imagine she had anything to do with this, but you understand why I had to ask, don't you?"

Janice nodded, though her eyes were still narrowed, calculating.

"Thank you again, Janice, and please keep this to yourself for the time being."

"I certainly will, Warden Barnes. You can count on me."

Once in the corridor headed back to his office, Henry said to Lewis, "That was a waste of time."

"What do you want to do now?"

"I think we definitely need to cover our bases and speak to Ms. Webster."

"I'll call her."

Henry paused. He glanced up and down the corridor as if ensuring it was just the two of them. "We're not going to call her."

Lewis frowned. "What do you mean?"

"If we call her now and she *is* involved, we'll only her tip her off. No, I'll speak to Maryann Webster personally."

"I'm not sure that's a good idea, sir."

"Lewis, I've been at Wrightsville for almost forty years. I've been the warden for sixteen of those years. I'm sixty-two years old and very close to retirement. I'll tell you, I want my retirement to happen here. They're going to transfer me once this is all over, if not outright fire me. There's a good chance I'll lose my pension. The only thing I have going for me right now is to try to fix this. Granted, my reputation is already tarnished, but if Maryann Webster *is* somehow involved in this, then maybe this is my way of saving some face."

Just like Henry, Lewis looked up and down the hallway to make sure nobody was nearby. When he spoke, his deep voice became a whisper.

"What if she has nothing to with this? What if she's innocent in this whole thing?"

"Then I'll thank her for her time, no harm done."

Lewis was quiet for a moment, considering it. He shook his head. "I don't think this is a good idea."

"None of it's a good idea, but what other choice do I have?"

"Maybe she was in on it," Lewis said. "Maybe she met them somewhere outside as their getaway."

"There's only one way to find out. I'm going to make a house call."

"At four o'clock in the morning?"

Henry shrugged. "More reason for her to be home, don't you think?"

"This falls on me now too," Lewis said.

"No, it doesn't. You brought the information to me. I told you I would contact the proper authorities. As far as you're concerned, that's what I did."

For a moment, there was a silence.

"No," Lewis said, "I don't think I can let you do that."

Henry's jaw tightened. "Lewis—"

"I don't think I can let you go by yourself. What if Maryann Webster *does* have something to do with this? No, I'm coming with you."

5

The driver inserted the debit card into the drive-thru ATM. He glanced back at Ashley, asked, "What's the PIN?"

She said nothing.

The man beside her growled, "Tell him the fucking PIN."

Ashley told him the four numbers and then blurted, "Please, I don't have that much."

The driver punched the numbers in the ATM. He hit the button for balance inquiry and waited a moment for the system to load her account.

"She's not kidding," the driver said. "She only has three hundred twenty-seven dollars in her checking."

"Shit," said the man beside her.

The driver leaned back out the window and hit WITHDRAW and typed in $300 and then waited for the machine to spit out the bills. Seconds later they were moving again, out of the bank parking lot, back onto the highway.

"Three hundred bucks," the man beside her muttered. "How much did you get from the gas station register?"

"Barely eighty dollars."

"Shit. Just how far are we going to go with three hundred eighty bucks?"

The driver glanced again at the debit card. He grazed his thumb over the raised letters and said, "Ashley Gilmore." He eyed her in the rearview mirror. "Nice to meet you, Ashley Gilmore."

She said nothing, redirecting her focus out her window.

The man beside her said, "Shit, that's right. We never introduced ourselves. Where are our manners?" He barked out a laugh which caused Ashley to cringe. "My name's Sean Wescott. That up there is Neal Palmer. Maybe you've heard of us?"

Again Ashley made no reply.

The driver, Neal Palmer, said, "Ashley, what's your kid's name?"

Silence.

"Ashley, I know it's hard to believe, but we're not going to hurt you."

"Well," Sean said, "we can't really make that promise." He leaned in close to her, his body pressing against hers. "We can certainly say our intention is not to hurt you, but whether or not you end up getting hurt in the end is not really up to us. It's not really up to you, either, though I'd say if you do what we tell you, the better shot you have of getting out of this in one piece."

Still staring out her window, watching the houses and trees whip past, Ashley said nothing.

"So your baby," Neal said, "is it is a girl or a boy?"

Ashley was quiet for a long couple of seconds, and then she answered in a soft voice.

"Boy."

"What's his name?"

She jerked her attention to the front. "Why do you need to know his name?"

"I don't," Neal said. "Just trying to have a conversation with you."

"I don't want to have a conversation with you. I don't even want to be here. Why are you *doing* this to me?"

Her voice had begun to quiver, and she wiped at fresh tears brimming her eyes.

Sean said, "Just wrong place, wrong time. Ain't that the way it always goes?" He was quiet for a moment. "Do you even have the slightest clue who we are?"

She looked away again, out her window, and nodded. "You're the two from the news. The ones who escaped the prison."

Sean chuckled. "That we are. That we are."

Ahead of them, farther down the highway, headlights appeared. Soon those headlights grew larger until a tractor-trailer tore past them in the opposite lane, its driver completely oblivious to the two escapees in the Mazda.

Neal eyed Ashley in the rearview mirror. "Who's watching him?"

She frowned. "What?"

"Your boy."

"My boyfriend," she said. She nearly spat the words, and once she started it didn't seem like she could stop. "He's a cop. He's going to realize something is wrong when I don't get home and he's going to get the rest of his cop friends together and they're going to track you both down."

For an instant, neither man spoke, both stunned. Then Sean barked out a laugh again, actually slapping his knee.

"Good one," he said. "You had me going for a second, but obviously it's bullshit. Tell us who's watching your boy."

She was quiet for another moment, staring out her window, before she whispered, "My mother."

Sean touched his ear, tilted his head toward her. "Say that again?"

"My mother is watching him. She watches him most nights I work late."

Sean glanced up at Neal.

Neal said, "Get her cell phone."

Sean picked up her purse, started digging through it. He pulled out an iPhone. "Should we have her call her mother?"

Neal was silent for a moment, adjusting his glasses. "See if she regularly texts with her mom first."

Sean powered on the phone, tried to access the main menu but the screen was locked. He handed it to Ashley.

"Unlock it."

At first, it didn't seem like she was even going to take the phone from him, but then she did, her hand trembling as she entered the passcode.

Sean took the phone back and began browsing through it.

"Well?" Neal said.

"Yeah, it looks like she texts with her mom on a pretty regular basis."

"Shoot her a text. Tell her Ashley won't be home any time soon."

Sean typed in a quick text, reading it aloud: "'Have to stay late. Will be home ASAP.'" He said to Neal, "Good enough?"

"Should be."

"Sent," Sean said.

There was a long minute of silence, just the purr of the Mazda's tires on the highway.

The iPhone chimed.

"Ah, here we go," Sean said. "Mommy responded with a simple 'Okay. Be safe. Love you.'"

"Love you too," Sean said slowly as he typed on the phone, and then hit send. He said to Neal, "Now what?"

"Turn it off and toss it."

"What do you mean?"

Neal eyed him in the rearview mirror. "Once the authorities realize she's been abducted, they're going to try to track her phone. You want them to know where we are?"

"Good point," Sean said. He powered off the phone, lowered his window, and tossed it outside.

A distressed noise—a sort of screech—emitted from Ashley's throat as she turned in her seat to stare out the rear window.

"Relax," Sean said. "It's just a fucking phone."

"There are pictures of my son on it."

"Oh," Sean said. "Well, I'm sure you have other pictures of him."

She glared at him now, her face full of fury. "You bastard."

"Hey!" Sean jabbed a finger at her face. "This isn't a game. You better watch your fucking mouth."

He grabbed the purse again, shoved his hand inside, and pulled out her driver's license.

"Here we go," Sean said, staring down at her picture on the ID. "Now we have your address, so if you decide to do something stupid, we know exactly where to go to find your son."

Ashley said nothing, trembling again.

Sean handed the ID up to Neal, said, "Keep this safe for now, okay?"

Neal took the ID, slipped it into his jeans pocket. He said, "Where to now?"

"Keep heading north."

"You're going to have to give me a specific location sooner or later."

"I realize that, but for now keep heading north."

Ashley asked, "Where are you taking me?"

"Don't you worry about it, honey." Sean placed his hand on her thigh, causing her to jerk as if she'd just been shocked.

Neal watched Sean in the rearview mirror. Sean grinning at the reaction he'd just gotten from the girl. Then glancing up front, noticing Neal watching him, and giving him a wink.

"Daylight will be here soon," Neal said. "We're going to have to find a place to hole up."

"Just keep driving," Sean said. "We'll find a place."

Ashley said, "But what if—"

She stopped at once.

Sean said, "What if what?"

She shook her head.

Sean placed his hand on her thigh, gave it a slight squeeze. To her credit, Ashley didn't jerk this time.

"Tell us, sugar."

Ashley looked up front again, met Neal's gaze in the rearview mirror. Her gaze shifted toward Sean, back to Neal, then back out her window.

She said, "What if the police catch up to us?"

"Why, sugar"—Sean leaned into her again, his voice dropping to a low whisper—"that's why you're here. You're our hostage."

6

"We need gas."

The man in the back with her, Sean, said, "How low are we?"

"Only a quarter tank," the driver said, "but I don't want to wait too long to fill up."

They were still on the highway, headed north. It was just after five o'clock in the morning.

With every car that passed them in the opposite lane, Ashley tensed as if somehow that car's driver would notice her trapped in the Mazda and save her.

Sean said, "There should be a gas station coming up soon, right?"

There was. Four miles later they went around a curve and a gas station glowed in the distance.

Neal eased into the parking lot and parked at the farthest pump. Ashley caught a snatch of Muzak when he stepped out of the car. He had her debit card with him and he swiped it in the machine and waited for a beat, just standing there, before his shoulders fell and he turned and opened the back door and leaned his head in.

"What's the problem?" Sean said.

"Machine says I have to go inside."

"Shit." Sean gazed out the front of the Mazda at the minimart several yards away. There were no other cars in the parking lot. Just one clerk inside. "You want to try another station?"

Neal thought about it for a moment, his fingers tapping the car's hood, and shook his head. "I'll go inside, pay cash."

"You sure?"

Now Neal gazed at the minimart too. Stared for a long moment and nodded and said, "Yeah, I'll be right back."

"How about grabbing a six-pack?"

Neal ducked his head back down, stared hard at Sean.

Sean shrugged. "Haven't had any beer in two years. I'm thirsty. Grab some cigarettes too."

They watched Neal stride across the parking lot to the minimart. He went inside, stepped up to the counter, spoke to the old woman clerk. As he did this, headlights splashed the Mazda as another car entered the parking lot.

"Fuck," Sean whispered.

Ashley tensed.

Sean said, "Stay calm."

A police cruiser parked in front of the minimart. A police officer of considerable size climbed out. The officer glanced their way. He stared for a moment and then turned and started for the minimart's entrance.

"Fuck," Sean said again.

They could see Neal finishing up at the counter. He turned, a six-pack of beer at his side, and started for the door. He turned back, said something to the old woman, and then continued on toward the exit.

Just as the police officer opened the door.

Neal paused. Stood completely still for an instant, and then motioned for the cop to enter. The cop shook his head, motioned for Neal to exit first. Neal nodded, said thank you, and stepped outside, the cop holding open the door long enough for Neal to pass by.

Neal didn't look back as he made a beeline straight for the Mazda.

A moment later he opened Ashley's door and handed in the six-pack of beer and tossed in two packs of cigarettes.

"Budweiser?" Sean said, wrinkling his nose.

Neal ignored him, slamming the door shut and reaching for the gas tank. It took two minutes to run through twenty dollars of gas, and then Neal replaced the pump and replaced the cap and glanced once more toward the minimart.

The cop stood at the counter—no, leaning on the counter—talking to the woman. Bullshitting.

Neal got back in the Mazda and started the engine.

Sean said, "Let's get the fuck out of here."

Neal put the car in gear, got them rolling forward. Without moving his lips too much, he asked, "Why didn't you two duck behind the seats?"

"I thought about it," Sean said, "but what if that cop had approached the car, looked inside? Would have been worse."

Neal said nothing as he steered them out of the parking lot and back on the highway.

Sean said, "What did that woman ask you on your way out?"

"She asked if I wanted a book of matches."

"That was thoughtful of her."

Neal let out a heavy sigh, checking the rearview mirror to make sure the police cruiser wasn't following. He pressed his foot hard on the gas, putting as much distance between them and the cop as he could.

7

After several miles, Ashley cleared her throat and found her voice to ask a question.

"How did that cop not recognize you?"

Sean barked out a laugh.

Ashley looked at him, then up at Neal. "What's so funny?"

"Nothing," Sean said. "Well, no, I guess that's not true. See, the picture they're showing of us on the news? That's not what we look like now."

"What do you mean?"

"Those mug shots," Sean said, "they're typical mug shots. I got a beard in mine, Neal's got a goatee. We got long hair in them too. Mine's curly, Neal's is straighter."

She looked back and forth from both men. "You ... neither of you has facial hair."

Sean grinned, nodding his head. "That's right. The first thing we did once we got out was shave them. Our hair too. Shit, those glasses Neal's wearing? He doesn't even wear glasses. They're fake."

"How ... how did you escape?"

"Through a hole in the wall in our cell," Sean said and laughed again. "Neal's the one who figured it out. He's the one who put the plan into motion. Me, I just hitched a ride."

Neal eyed Sean in the rearview mirror but said nothing.

Sean's smile dropped off his face. He said, "You'll get your money, I swear."

Ashley said, "What money?"

"Don't worry about it," Sean said. He grabbed the knife beside him and inspected the blade in the dark. Ashley couldn't tell if there was anything on it, but he wiped both sides of the blade off on the seat.

"How did you cut your hair?" Ashley asked.

The smile returned to Sean's face again. He beamed. "That's the genius part. We had someone on the inside. Managed to get us some supplies. She had a truck waiting for us with clothes and a razor, even a few packs of cigarettes."

"Who is she?"

Sean reached out and touched Ashley's face, running his thumb over her cheek. "Don't you worry about it, sugar."

Ashley jerked away, leaned as far back against her door as was humanly possible. "If you had a truck, why did you—" Her voice broke, and she began to sob again.

"Abduct you?" Sean frowned. "Weren't you listening earlier? You're our hostage."

She wiped at the tears in her eyes. "But why *me?*"

"'Why me, why me, why me?'" Sean mimicked. He leaned close to her, his breath hot on her face, a raw intensity in his eyes. "Why not you?"

"Hey," Neal said from up front. "Knock it off."

Sean didn't move, still leaning into her. His hand moved across her leg and up to her breast where it gave a slight squeeze.

"Two years without beer, two years without pussy. Can make a man go insane."

Ashley trembled beneath his touch. "Please," she whispered. "Please don't."

"'Please don't,'" Sean mimicked again. He stared hard at her for a beat, then barked out another laugh, ran his tongue over her cheek, and sat back on his side of the seat.

Neal eyed him in the rearview mirror again.

Sean said, "What the fuck is your problem?"

"You wanted to ditch the truck and get a hostage, we ditched the truck and got a hostage. But we need that hostage to be alive."

"She is alive."

"We also need her to be compliant."

Sean leered at Ashley. "We'll see about that later."

Ashley shuddered, hugging her arms over her chest.

Neal said, "I'm getting off the main highway. We've been on here too long as it is. Again, where the hell are we headed?"

"Just keep going north."

8

According to her employee file, Maryann Webster lived ten miles from the prison.

Henry and Lewis slowly drove past the house to check it out first. It looked peaceful enough.

All the lights were out.

Lewis said, "She's probably sleeping. Her car's right there."

A Chevy Malibu sat in the driveway.

They parked on the street, shutting their car doors quietly and walking up the driveway to the front door.

Henry whispered, "Should we knock?"

Lewis shook his head, slipping his cell phone from his pocket. "I saved the number from Maryann's file to my phone."

He pressed a button and put the phone to his ear.

Henry stood silent, his hands in the pockets of his jacket. It was another hour before sunrise. This early in the morning, the temperature was below freezing, enough so that he could see his breath. Somewhere nearby, wind chimes played a distant melody. No sound came from inside. No distant ringing. No cell phone vibrating on a bedside table.

Lewis closed his phone. "Voice mail."

"Now what?"

"I guess now you knock."

Henry knocked. He did it softly at first, but when there was no answer, he gave it more force.

Nothing.

"Maybe she's a deep sleeper," Henry said.

"Try the bell."

They heard the bell from outside, a low, sonorous ding-dong, but it elicited no answer.

"I got a bad feeling about this," Henry said.

Lewis took a step back, taking in the house as if for the first time. He did a slow three-sixty, scanning the other houses along the street, and then turned back to Henry.

"Try the door."

Henry did. Locked.

"We could circle the house," Lewis said. "See if there's a way around back."

"Go ahead. I'll wait here."

Lewis didn't look pleased to have to trespass on his own, but he went without a word. A minute later he circled around the other side of the house, shaking his head.

"I think we might as well get on with it," Lewis said.

"What do you mean?"

Lewis tilted his head at the door.

Henry stared at him for a beat. "You mean break *into* the house?"

"Hey, you were the one who wanted to come here. As far as we can tell, Maryann's car is in the driveway, which means she should be home. We knocked, we rang the doorbell, we called, but there has been no answer. After everything that's happened in the past twenty-four hours, I'd say we have some probable cause. But if it were me, I'd say let's do it around back."

Loose rocks bordered the walkway from the driveway to the

front door. Henry picked up a medium-sized rock, hefted it in his hand, and followed Lewis around to the back of the house. Here the door was mostly glass. Henry hesitated a beat before smashing the rock on the pane of glass closest to the deadbolt. He reached inside, flicked the lock, and pushed open the door.

They stepped over the shattered glass into the kitchen. An antiseptic smell hit them at once.

"Somebody's been cleaning," Lewis said. He pulled a flashlight from his pocket. Its beam swooped from one end of the house to the other.

Moving boxes were stacked everywhere. Many of them taped shut while others still looked like they were in the process of being filled.

They searched the house. It didn't take long. Maryann wasn't in the bedroom. She wasn't in any of the rooms on the first floor.

She was in the basement.

Henry was leaning against the counter in the kitchen when Lewis called up to him.

"You better come down here and see this."

Henry made his way down the steps, his left leg stiff from arthritis. He clutched the railing as he went, putting much of his focus on not tumbling forward. For a moment, he didn't see what Lewis was pointing the flashlight at. Then he turned, saw the pale face illuminated by the light, and sucked in air between his teeth.

"My God," he whispered.

Maryann Webster, hanging from the ceiling by a piece of wire wrapped around her neck, said nothing.

9

The local police arrived first, followed a while later by the state police.

Henry and Lewis gave their statements multiple times. None of the cops outright asked why they hadn't notified the police when they suspected something was amiss, but it was there right underneath the surface.

An hour had passed since they found Maryann Webster and still nobody had taken her down. They were waiting for a forensic detective to arrive before they could do that, one of the local guys said.

"It doesn't make sense," Henry said to Lewis in the living room, watching officers come and go through the house.

"What's that?"

"Why she would hang herself."

"She was feeling guilty. Knew she would get caught."

"But all the moving boxes ..." Henry shook his head. "I guess maybe the guilt got to be too much. Still, it doesn't make sense."

"How so?"

"Say she did help Palmer and Wescott and the guilt became too much. Why'd she kill herself? Why not turn herself in, try to make things right?"

"Maybe she knew there wasn't any point. Even if she did turn herself in, Palmer and Wescott were long gone by that point. Nothing she could have told the police would have helped bring them in."

Henry watched an officer with a bulky camera hurry through the front door and head to the basement.

"But what if," Henry said, though he left it at that.

Lewis glanced at him. "What if what?"

Henry shook his head. Then, reconsidering, "What if Palmer and Wescott came here, the first thing they did once they escaped? What if they murdered her?"

They were quiet for several long seconds, watching the officers.

Lewis asked one of them, "You still need us?"

The officer said, "You both headed home?"

"No," Lewis said, "back to the prison."

"That's fine. We have your contact information."

The officer disappeared back into the basement where Maryann Webster was still probably hanging from that wire.

Henry and Lewis left through the front door.

It was six o'clock in the morning now, the sun rising little by little over the horizon. Frosted dew covered the front lawn.

Five police cruisers were parked on the street and in the driveway. Two of them had their roof lights flashing, a kaleidoscope of blues and reds patterning the trees and nearby houses.

As Henry and Lewis headed down the driveway to their car, a news van arrived.

"Shit," Henry muttered. "I've had my fill of the news for the year."

"Just get in the car," Lewis said, pulling his keys from his pocket and hitting the button to unlock the vehicle.

Another state police cruiser pulled up as Henry was about to climb inside the car.

"Warden Barnes, I'm Lieutenant Marsh."

Henry paused, all too aware of the news crew setting up their location across the street. "Good morning, Lieutenant Marsh."

The trooper looked to be in his forties with a strong jaw and angular nose. He nodded at the house.

"You think she killed herself?"

Henry paused again.

Lieutenant Marsh said, his voice quiet, "A body was found forty miles from here. A gas station clerk's throat was cut. Whoever did it stuffed him in the trunk of his own car."

Henry glanced again at the crew across the street. The tripod had been set up while a kid who looked fresh out of high school hurriedly secured the camera on top. A young blonde reporter had a cell phone to her ear.

"Is there a connection to Palmer and Wescott?"

"Not sure," Lieutenant Marsh said. "But I wouldn't be surprised."

Henry checked the crew across the street again. Still nobody had recognized him. Or if they had, nobody cared.

"Are you headed there now?"

Lieutenant Marsh nodded. "I am. Heard about this before I left and wanted to swing by."

"Would you be opposed if I tagged along?"

Lieutenant Marsh dipped his head to glance at Lewis in the driver's seat. He said to Henry, "I wouldn't be opposed to it at all."

Henry told Lewis to go on without him and then walked around the cruiser to climb into the passenger side.

Before he closed his door, though, he heard the blonde reporter say, "Is that Warden Barnes?" She smacked the young cameraman on the arm. "Shit, why didn't you tell me Warden Barnes was here?"

"Go," Henry said, and as he clicked in his seat belt, Lieutenant Marsh accelerated down the street, leaving the news crew and Maryann Webster behind.

10

Five miles off the main highway, they came to a motel called the Green Valley Inn. Looked to be about a dozen rooms in all with the office positioned off to the side. A handful of cars were scattered about the parking lot. The vacancy sign under the motel's name was lit in bright red neon.

"What do you think?" Neal said, his foot off the gas, letting the Mazda coast forward.

Sean said, "I think it looks like a shit hole. But yeah, it'll do."

"The sun is just coming up now. Figure we should get off the road for a couple hours to regroup."

"Anything farther ahead on this road?"

Neal shook his head. "Not that I can remember."

"I thought you memorized the area."

"I did the best I could, but I'm still only human. I remembered that there was a motel here that looked out of the way. If we keep going, we'll meet up with another highway. Again, it would help to know exactly where we're headed."

"And again," Sean said, "all I'm gonna tell you is to keep going north."

Neal applied pressure to the brake, causing the Mazda to rock forward to a halt. Turning in his seat, he glared at Sean.

"Do you think this is a fucking joke?"

Sean only smiled.

"Every goddamned cop in this state is looking for us. In another day, every cop in the country will be looking for our faces. Now is not the time to fuck around."

Sean said nothing at first, just kept smiling. He glanced at Ashley, then said to Neal, "Forgive me if you don't think I'm taking this situation seriously. I'm taking it quite seriously. But keep in mind the level of money that we're talking about. If I tell you where it's located, you might just kill me so you can take all of it."

"How do I know the money even exists in the first place?"

Sean smiled again. "You don't."

The two men stared hard at each other for a long moment, then Neal turned back to the wheel.

They pulled into the parking lot, parked a few spaces away from the office. The lights were on inside, but nobody was currently stationed behind the counter.

"You want me to go in?" Sean asked.

"No way." Neal killed the engine, stared out the windshield at the empty office. "I'll go in."

"Take her too," Sean said, hooking a thumb at Ashley. "Make it less suspicious, like you're a couple."

Neal eyed Ashley in the rearview mirror. She sunk down in her seat as if making herself smaller might make her invisible.

"Listen here, sugar," Sean said, touching her leg again, "you're gonna go in there and you're gonna hold hands with Neal like you're a real goddamned couple. You're gonna make it look legit, because if you don't? We're gonna kill whoever shows up behind that counter, and then we're gonna head back to where you live and kill your mother and your boy. We're not gonna be quick about it either. We're gonna take our time with them, especially your boy, and believe me, it ain't gonna be pretty."

He squeezed her leg, hard enough to cause her to gasp, and he leaned in close so his lips were right by her ear.

"Got it?"

Trembling again, her entire body on edge, Ashley managed to nod.

"Then get going," Sean said, patting her lightly on the face.

There was no bell above the door, no way to signal their arrival. The place was spartan, just the counter and two office chairs. Framed pictures dotted the wall, what were probably snapshots of the surrounding area, all the frames in need of a good dusting.

A call bell sat on the counter.

Neal, gripping Ashley's hand, tapped the button on top to ring it.

For a solid minute, nothing happened.

Neal rang the bell again.

Shuffling sounded behind the door in back of the counter. The door creaked open and an old man peered out at them. He looked to be a wisp of a man, drowning in a dark flannel shirt. He yawned, wiped the sleep from his eyes, and stepped out to stand behind the counter.

"Morning," he murmured.

Neal said, "We'd like a room."

The old man barely even looked at them. He reached under the counter and brought up a register and started paging through to the most recent page.

"Don't get many people coming in at six thirty in the morning asking for a room," the old man said. "You been driving all night?"

"That we have," Neal said. "A bit exhausted."

"Well, check-in time is twelve noon, so if you plan on staying past that, I'll have to charge you two nights."

"How much is that?"

The man bit his lip, doing the math in his head. "That'll be one hundred forty dollars, plus tax."

Neal released Ashley's hand, dug into his pocket for the twenties from the ATM. He counted out eight of them and set them on the counter.

"Cash?" The old man looked surprised. "Thank God it's cash. I hate using that darned credit card machine. That's how the government tracks you, you know. That's why they invented credit cards. So they can get a running list of everything you buy, every place you've been, all of it. That's why I never use 'em. Never even signed up for one, to tell you the truth."

Neal and Ashley said nothing. Ashley stood a little too straight, too rigid. Neal reached over, placed his arm around her shoulder.

"You seem tense," he said. "You get that way when you're tired."

"And another thing the government does," the old man said, oblivious, his tone growing with outrage, "they put chemicals in the air. You ever see the stuff coming out of those big planes in the sky? They call them contrails, but that's not what they are. They're chemtrails. The government's been putting that shit in the air for decades now. Nobody can say what it is they hope to accomplish, but it's darned un-American, is what it is. If you don't believe me, just look for yourself next time you see one of them planes. It's true. I heard it on the radio."

Neal tapped the stack of twenties on the counter. "You said one hundred forty dollars plus tax, right?"

The man shook his head. "You think I'm crazy, don't you? Like I don't know what's really going on here. That's just what the government *wants* you to think. They don't want you to ask questions. They just want you to be good boys and girls and follow the rules."

"My girlfriend and I have been on the road for several hours tonight," Neal said. "We're both exhausted and just want to get some sleep."

The man sighed, clearly disappointed that his warnings were being ignored. "You'll see," he mumbled, scratching something in the register. "One of these days you'll see."

He opened a drawer, dug through several keys, and pulled out a key on a ring with a large fob that just said 9.

"One of you got an ID?"

Neal said, "Not with us. We left ours in the car."

The old man stared at them for a long moment, and then he grinned. "That's the spirit. IDs are just another form of Big Brother tracking your location. Good for you. But I will need to add a name to the book."

"John Butler," Neal said.

The old man took the twenties, slowly counted them out, then set them in the drawer and passed along the room key and change. "Now tomorrow you'll need to check out here at the office. We make people do that when they aren't using a credit card in case they damage the room. We just gotta inspect the room before you leave, and that's that. Won't take more than a few minutes. Otherwise, welcome to the Green Valley Inn. We hope you enjoy your stay."

11

Room 9 was even more spartan than the main office had been.

A single bed, tiny bedside table, lamp, TV, and chair. That was it. No pictures on the wall.

Sean opened the bedside table drawer. "Not even a Gideon bible," he said, and slammed the drawer shut and wandered into the bathroom.

Ashley stood motionless, her hands clasped in front of her.

"Why don't you have a seat," Neal said.

Ashley walked over to the chair and sank down into it, her nose crinkling at the smell.

Neal set the six-pack aside, grabbed the remote, and turned on the TV. He skimmed through the channels until he found basic cable news. CNN, MSNBC, Fox News. Only CNN was showing live coverage this early in the morning.

The toilet flushed, the sink went, and then Sean emerged from the bathroom. He had a white towel in his hand. "Anything new?"

Neal gestured at the towel. "What are you doing with that?"

Sean slipped the switchblade from his pocket. He ejected the blade and used it to start tearing the towel into long strips. He pointed the knife at Ashley.

"Get on the bed."

Her eyes widened.

"Sean," Neal said.

Sean ignored him.

"Get on the fucking bed."

He grabbed her arm and yanked her from the chair, pushed her onto the bed.

She struggled, and he slapped her across the face.

"Relax," he said. "I'm just gonna tie you to the bed to make sure you don't get any crazy ideas."

"Wait," Neal said. "Maybe she needs to use the bathroom."

Sean paused, considering this. He asked Ashley, "You need to use the john?"

Tears had brimmed her eyes again. She nodded.

Sean leaned back and pointed at the bathroom. "Then get to it."

Ashley scrambled off the bed. She hustled into the bathroom, started to the shut the door, but Sean was there, blocking it from closing entirely.

"I don't think so," he said. "Leave it open."

"But—"

"Leave it open or don't use the bathroom at all."

She nodded, her shoulders down, defeated.

"Relax," Sean said. "Nobody's gonna watch you."

Sean turned his back to the bathroom, focused on the TV as he pulled out a cigarette and lit it.

Neal and Sean's mug shots flashed on the screen again. Both with long hair, Sean a beard, Neal a goatee.

The picture switched to show a house in a residential area. Cop cars everywhere. On the screen flashed the words POSSI-BLE ACCOMPLICE?

Sean said, "They catch her?"

Neal said nothing, watching the TV.

A reporter on the scene spoke into a microphone. She said, "We aren't getting too many details at the moment, but what we do know is that a woman was found dead in this home not too long ago."

"Dead?" Sean looked around for an ashtray, didn't see one, and tapped the ash on the TV stand.

The reporter continued, "At this time authorities have not made an official statement, but we have been able to confirm that the woman was an employee of Wrightsville Correctional Facility until Wednesday."

In the bathroom, the toilet flushed.

Sean leaned back to watch Ashley wash her hands. When she stepped out of the bathroom, he pointed at the bed.

"I won't run," she said, her voice nearly a plea.

Sean said, "Don't make me tell you again."

Ashley crossed over to the bed. Before she sat down on it, though, Sean told her to wait. He took one of the strips of the towel, placed it in her mouth, and tied the ends behind her head.

"Not perfect," he said, "but it'll do."

He had her lie down on the bed and tied her wrists to the headboard. Then he stepped back, nodded to himself at a job well done. "I could use a beer. Neal, you want a beer?"

Neal kept his focus on the TV. "I'm okay."

"Come on," Sean said, "you need a beer."

He grabbed a can, popped the top, and handed it to Neal.

Sean popped the top of his own, took a long swallow. "I don't know about you, but I'd say we deserve a beer after what we managed to pull off."

"I feel like you're not taking this seriously."

Sean took another long swallow, watching Neal from the corner of his eye. He set the beer aside, took another drag from his cigarette.

"You don't think I'm taking this seriously?"

"That's what I said."

"Fuck you. You have no idea just how serious I am."

Neal set the beer on the TV stand next to the pile of ash. "If you were taking this seriously, you would be honest with me about the money."

"I told you, I'm not ready to tell you yet."

"When?"

"When the time's right."

Neal shook his head. "This is bullshit."

"If you had one and a half million dollars stashed away, would you just tell any Joe Shmoe who asked where it's located?"

"You still view me as a Joe Shmoe?"

"Don't get me wrong, Neal, I appreciate what you've done. I told you I'd take care of you and I mean it. You'll get your cut."

Neal glanced at Ashley, who lay motionless on the bed, the towel in her mouth, watching them.

"You better not touch her."

Sean grinned. "Why—you got a thing for her?"

"The only reason we abducted her was to use as a hostage. We agreed on that point when you came up with the stupid idea."

"I wouldn't say my idea was stupid."

"She's a risk, Sean. Before it was only the two of us. Now we have to keep an eye on her twenty-four-seven."

"But if the cops catch up with us, we use her as leverage."

"The idea is that the cops *won't* catch up with us."

Sean drained his beer, turned to grab another one.

Neal said, "I think you've had enough."

"Fuck what you think." Sean crushed out his cigarette, popped the top on his second beer and took a long swallow. "What's your fucking problem, anyway?"

"We're the two most wanted men in the state, and you're acting like this is all one big game."

"Is it that dead bitch?" Sean asked, pointing at the TV. "They won't publicly announce it any time soon, but how much you want to bet she offed herself?"

CNN had since gone to a commercial break, but the meaning was clear enough.

Sean said, "You had a thing for her, didn't you? You were pissed when she didn't show."

"She had said she might not."

"And now"—Sean shook his head, taking another swallow of beer—"now she's dead. That's on you, Neal."

"Shut up."

"I don't know what you're so upset about. She got us out. That's all we needed her for."

"I said shut up."

"Who knows," Sean said, "maybe she left a note saying how it was all your fault. That—"

Neal's fist caught Sean off guard. He stumbled back, dropped his can, the beer soaking the carpet.

"What the motherfuck?" Sean touched the side of his face where Neal's fist had connected. "You really don't want your cut, do you?"

"I'm getting tired of your shit."

"Half a million dollars," Sean said, "and you're willing to give it all away over some cunt."

Neal's glare burned into Sean. "If you want to go back to prison, be my guest."

Sean just stood there for a moment, watching Neal. Then his face broke and he barked out a laugh.

"That's the spirit. Finally, you got some fire in your eyes." Sean tilted his head at Ashley on the bed. "Wanna have the first go?"

Neal raised a finger at him. "You're not touching her."

Sean laughed again. "I'm just playing with you. But seriously, you're cranky. When was the last time you slept? Maybe you should get some shut-eye."

"I'm fine. Besides, we shouldn't stay here too long, just a couple hours. Steal another car if we can. No telling how long before she's reported missing and the cops start looking for the Mazda."

"Sit down in that chair, close your eyes." Sean grabbed Neal's beer off the TV stand, handed it to him. "Some sleep could do you good."

"I'm fine," Neal repeated, but he wandered over to the chair and sat down anyway.

Sean grabbed the remote off the bed, started skimming through the channels. "I wonder if they have any decent porn."

The towels strips around Ashley's wrists were too tight. She struggled for a second until Sean glared back at her and then she went all at once still and silent.

Neal took a sip of his beer. He watched the TV as Sean flipped through the channels, his eyelids growing heavier and heavier until he closed his eyes completely.

12

It was seven o'clock in the morning by the time they arrived at the gas station. A handful of police cars were already on the scene.

Lieutenant Marsh pulled into the lot and killed the engine. Henry took an extra moment to stretch his legs before getting out.

A small crowd of cops had formed around the car behind the minimart. Someone was taking pictures of the car.

Lieutenant Marsh asked one of the cops, "You guys think this was from the escapees?"

One of the local cops, a sergeant, blew into his hands to warm them. "Whoever did it took the surveillance hard drive, so that's gone."

"No witnesses?"

"None that we've found. Judging by the body, we think he was killed around two, three o'clock, which gives a window of about four hours at least."

"How was he found?"

"A trucker pulled in around five o'clock. He's a regular, apparently, always chats with the night clerk before starting his day and thought it was strange all the lights were out. He noticed the car was still parked in the back, got suspicious, and called the police. When the patrol officer arrived, she checked the car and found the body in the trunk."

The trunk lid was half-closed, obscuring any view of the body. Still a small pool of blood had spread on the pavement underneath the trunk like an oil stain.

Lieutenant Marsh said, "So no idea who did this and where they went?"

The sergeant shook his head. "Again, the surveillance hard drive was taken."

Henry stepped away for a moment, turning his back on the blood and the dead body and how it had been so cruelly shoved into the tight space. He took a deep breath, trying to settle his nerves, and stared across the highway at the bank.

He asked, "What about the bank?"

The sergeant said, "What about it? It's closed for another half hour."

"But the ATM—it looks right out onto the highway, right over here. What if it managed to catch what happened?"

The bank manager met them in the vestibule where the ATM was located facing the parking lot, its camera staring out through the glass window, out across the parking lot and across the highway at the gas station.

"So it was Seth, huh?" The bank manager shook his head. "Didn't know him very well, only saw him occasionally, but he seemed like a nice enough kid. Even had an account here. Damned shame."

"How can we access the security feed?" Lieutenant Marsh asked.

The bank manager sighed. "Unfortunately, that's a corporate decision. I need to contact my regional manager and the head of security and explain what's happened and what you're requesting. There's a chance they may request you present a warrant, but I think under the circumstances they'll agree to give you access to the footage." He slipped a cell phone from his jacket pocket. "Let me just make a quick call and I'll be right back."

It wasn't just one quick call the bank manager had to make, but five. First the regional manager, then the head of security, *then* the regional manager again, before waiting for a call from the district manager, and then finally calling the head of security again, before the bank manager was given official permission to allow the police to examine the security footage.

They waited in the back office, standing around the computer as the security footage was uploaded from the corporate office back to the bank.

"They already reviewed the footage at corporate," the bank manager said. "I'm told the incident occurred around three o'clock. They still sent along footage starting at midnight in case anything leading up to the incident will help."

The bank manager moved the mouse around on the screen and got the footage to fast-forward to close to three o'clock in the morning. The gas station was empty until a sedan pulled into the parking lot and parked on the side of the building. The quality of the footage wasn't good for the distance, but they were able to see a young woman step out of the car and make her way inside. Five minutes passed before she reappeared, and during that time two men had taken up position near the car, dark figures in the night. They looked inside the car, talked for a time, and then moved away. One of the figures stood in the shadows while the other one ducked behind the car.

What happened next happened quickly. The woman reappeared, and as she approached the car, the figure standing in the shadows approached her. She turned, startled, and as she did the figure hiding behind the car ran up and pressed something against her throat.

"A knife," Lieutenant Marsh said.

The sergeant said, "How can you tell?"

"If it was a pistol, he'd press it against her back."

One of the men opened the back door and started to push the woman into the backseat when the clerk appeared at the edge of the frame. When the clerk realized what had happened, he turned and ran. One of the men gave chase and brought him right back. The man with the knife stepped out of the car, spoke to the other man, and then thrust the blade into the clerk's stomach. That was when the girl exited the car and ran out of frame. The man with the knife chased after her. The two reappeared, the man with the knife shoving the girl back in the car, and then he approached the other man and the clerk who now lay on the ground. The two men spoke briefly again, and then the man with the knife leaned down and sliced the clerk's throat. The two men then dragged him out of frame to presumably put the clerk in the trunk of his own car.

While the man with the knife stood by the car, the first man disappeared from frame as he ran inside the minimart. A minute later all the lights went out and the man reappeared holding the security hard drive. The two men got into the car, the one with the knife climbing into the back along with the girl, and they drove off headed north.

"My God," Henry murmured. He looked around at the other men. "She's been abducted."

13

Despite the strip of towel in her mouth, Ashley screamed as loud as she could.

All that came out was a strained, gargled cry. Not loud enough for anybody to hear outside this room. It barely woke Neal, who was slumped in the chair, asleep.

"Shh," Sean said, kneeling over her, his hands running up and down her body. "Just be a good girl and stay quiet."

Ashley screamed again. Her arms were bound to the bed, yes, but her legs were free. She kicked at Sean though it did little good. He pressed his weight down on her legs, holding her in place, leaning even closer to her, his breath hot and reeking of beer and cigarettes.

"Don't fight it," he whispered. "You don't want me to get the knife."

Ashley screamed once again.

In the chair, Neal stirred awake. He raised his head, his eyes narrow at first, but when he saw what Sean was doing, his eyes snapped open and he jumped to his feet.

Sean was aware of movement off to the side, but before he

could do anything about it, Neal had grabbed him by the back of his neck and yanked him off the bed.

"What the fuck are you doing?" Neal said.

Sean stumbled toward the wall. He had to grab it to stay balanced. He kept his back to Neal and Ashley, a low chuckle building in the base of his throat. Finally he barked out a laugh and turned, grinning at Neal.

"I told you I missed beer and I missed pussy. I got my beer, so now the only thing I need is pussy."

Neal glanced at the empty beer cans littering the floor.

"I told you not to get drunk."

Sean waved this aside. "Fuck you."

"Do you want to get caught? Because you're acting like someone who wants to get his ass put back in a cell."

Sean's lazy smile turned all at once severe. His glare burned into Neal.

"What I want," he breathed, "is to bust a nut. And I'm going to fucking do that."

"No, you're not."

Still glaring at Neal, Sean slipped the switchblade from his pocket.

Neal said, "Don't do anything stupid."

Sean hit the button on the side, letting the blade pop up with an almost silent *snick*.

Neal placed himself between Sean and Ashley. "You're not going to touch her."

Sean held the knife at his side. Didn't say anything, just kept glaring back at Neal.

On the bed, Ashley trembled now with fear, her entire body quivering. Tears brimmed her eyes.

For a moment, there was silence besides the low drone of the TV. Neal noted that the time was nine o'clock. He'd been asleep for just two hours.

Sean said, "Do you want to die?"

Neal made no reply.

"I have no problem killing you. I just want you to understand that. I don't care that you helped get me out of Wrightsville. I don't care that I promised you half a million dollars. In fact, no, I do care, because if I kill you then that's an extra half a million for me. So really, now that I'm thinking about it, I'm asking myself why *don't* I kill you?"

"You're drunk. We need to stay focused."

"No," Sean said. "*We* don't need to do anything. *You* need to get out of my fucking way."

Neal held his ground. "You're not touching her."

"Oh, I plan on doing much more than touching her."

Ashley sobbed quietly on the bed.

Sean said, "What are you going to do, Neal? Are you going to call the police?" He barked out another laugh. "Go ahead. I'm sure they'd love to hear from you."

Neal said nothing.

"Or"—Sean held up the knife—"are you going to take this from me? Because I'd *love* to see you try."

Again Neal said nothing.

Sean smiled. "Half a million dollars. Are you really going to give up half a million dollars over this stupid bitch?"

When Neal still didn't answer, Sean said, "Wait—do you have a thing for her? Is that what this is about? If that's the case, then you can go after me." Another grin. "Just hope you don't mind sloppy seconds."

On the bed, Ashley continued to sob.

Sean dropped the knife to his side. "If you think you can take this blade from me, go ahead and try."

Neal didn't move.

Sean's eyes turned dark. He snarled, "Say something!"

Neal took a deep breath. He stood frozen for a long moment, then turned and looked down at Ashley.

"I'm sorry," he said.

She cried out again, her entire body shaking.

"Wise decision," Sean said.

Neal didn't answer. He walked to the door. Placed his hand on the knob. Stood there for an extra second, as if debating with himself, before he opened the door and stepped out into the morning sunlight.

As the door closed, Sean set the knife on the bedside table and smiled down at Ashley, unbuckling his belt.

"Now," he said, "where were we?"

14

He stood frozen on the walkway outside Room 9 for several seconds, staring out at the parking lot. His heart was pounding. Adrenaline still coursed through his blood. He breathed slowly, trying to settle his heart. At one point he turned back to the door, reached for the doorknob, but shook his head. Stood frozen again for another several seconds before he headed toward the office.

A pay phone was positioned just outside the building. It didn't look like it had been serviced in years. In fact, the thing barely looked like it worked at all. Probably a relic of a time when cell phones didn't exist and nobody had bothered to dismantle it and take it to the junkyard. Still, he lifted the receiver and placed it to his ear to see whether there was a ringtone.

Nothing.

He replaced the receiver and headed into the office. Unlike before, somebody was stationed behind the counter. Only this somebody was not the old man with the wild conspiracy theories.

"Help you?"

The kid couldn't have been older than eighteen years old. Not a kid, exactly, but he clearly tried to make himself look older than he really was. Facial hair dotted his chin in what was apparently supposed to pass as a goatee.

"Can I use the phone?"

The kid peered at him over the counter. "There's a pay phone outside."

"It doesn't work."

"You don't got a cell phone?"

"No."

The kid glanced past him, as if searching for a car. "You even have a room here?"

"Yes."

"Then why don't you use the phone in there?"

"My girlfriend's sleeping." He kept his gaze steady with the kid's. "Am I able to use the phone in here? I'm assuming you have one right there behind the counter."

"Well, yeah, maybe I do. But I still don't understand why you can't use the phone in your room."

"Where's the gentleman that helped me earlier?"

"You mean Pops?"

"He's your grandfather?"

"No, but he's so old everybody calls him Pops. He always works the late shift."

"How much?"

The kid frowned. "What do you mean?"

"To use the phone you have behind the counter. How much do you want?"

The kid studied him for several long seconds, trying to decide whether or not it was a serious question. Finally he said, "Twenty bucks."

"Fine." He pulled the wad of twenties from his pocket. Extracted one, placed it on the counter.

"Changed my mind," the kid said. "Let's make it forty."

He just stared at him.

"Hey"—the kid shrugged—"it's the power of supply and demand. Besides, I see you're not hurting for cash. I could ask for sixty."

He took the twenty off the counter, stuffed it back in his pocket. He turned to leave.

"Fine," the kid said. "Let's meet in the middle and call it thirty."

He walked to the door.

The kid said, "What room did you say you were in again?"

He didn't answer, pushing through the door and stepping outside, his left hand balled into so tight a fist that the fingernails dug into his skin.

15

Ryan waited until the guy had been gone a couple seconds before he moved out from behind the counter and walked up to the window to peer outside.

The guy was in the parking lot now, his head down, pacing back and forth.

What was he waiting for?

After a minute, the guy made his way up to the walkway, stationed himself in front of Room 9, and just stared out at the road.

Ryan headed back to the counter. He pushed through the door into the back room and sat down at the computer.

He opened Internet Explorer and brought up Fox News's webpage, which featured the two men who had escaped Wrightsville Correctional Facility yesterday. On the main page were the two men's mug shots, no doubt taken years ago, but still they were clear enough.

At the top of the screen were the words BREAKING: POSSIBLE ACCOMPLICE FOUND DEAD.

Ryan clicked on the link. He scanned the text, found that it was about a nurse at the prison who may have helped the two men escape.

He clicked back to the main page, stared at the mug shots.

Ryan focused on Neal Palmer.

In the photo, Neal had a goatee and long hair. The guy who had just been out in the office—and who was probably still loitering outside Room 9—didn't have a goatee or long hair. In the mug shot, Neal wasn't wearing glasses, while the guy who had wanted to use the phone had worn glasses.

Ryan squinted at the mug shot for several long seconds before he leaned back in his chair. Put his hands to his face, rubbed his eyes, and then leaned forward again, focusing on the photo.

He shot up from the chair and hurried back out into the main office. Crept up to the window again and peered out through the dusty pane.

The guy was still stationed outside Room 9, his one foot up on the railing. Didn't look like he had moved at all.

Ryan returned to the counter. He opened the drawer, took out the register, and flipped to the most recent page. Last night Pops had scribbled in the name John Butler for Room 9. That was it. Nothing else in the drawer. No Xerox of John Butler's driver's license. No credit card receipt. Pops had just left a notation beside the name: *Cash*.

He tossed the register back into the drawer, slammed it shut. Picked up his cell phone on the counter. He held it in his hand for a long beat, staring at the blank screen, before he hit the home button and the screen lit up and he put in his passcode and brought up the phone application.

He dialed Brett.

The phone rang three times and then went to voice mail.

Ryan disconnected the call.

A moment later the phone vibrated with an incoming text message from Brett.

AT WORK WHAT'S UP?

Ryan typed back: CALL ME ASAP.

The phone in hand, Ryan returned to peek back out the window.

The guy was still standing outside Room 9.

The phone vibrated again, this time with an incoming call.

Ryan said, "You need to leave work right now."

"What are you talking about?"

"You remember those two guys who escaped Wrightsville?"

"I think so."

"One of them's here."

Silence.

Ryan said, "Brett, are you there?"

Brett cleared his throat. "Listen, dude, I'm already on thin ice here at work. They wrote me up last week for—"

"We need to get Blake and George out here too. Bring the pickups and the guns."

Brett was quiet for another beat. "Dude, what the fuck are you thinking? Call the police."

"The police show up, there's no reward."

Another beat of silence.

Brett said, "There's a reward?"

"Of course there's a reward. At least, I can't imagine they wouldn't give us something."

"So call the police. You'll still get the reward."

"Dude, think how much pussy we'll get if we're the ones who bring them in?"

Brett was silent for a moment. He said, "But how sure are you one of them's even there?"

Ryan peeked out the window again. As he did, the door to Room 9 opened. Another man stood there, wearing only boxer shorts. The guy turned away from the railing. He stared at the man inside the room. The man in the boxer shorts walked away, leaving the door open. The guy didn't move at first, just stood there, and then he walked in and closed the door behind him.

"Not just one," Ryan said. "Both of them. Shit, dude, this is the real deal."

Brett was quiet for another moment. Then he said, "Fuck it. I'll call Blake and George. We'll be there as soon as possible."

16

Neal stepped into the room.

Ashley was on the bed, her arms still bound to the headboard, her mouth still gagged. She was sobbing. A sheet covered her body. Her scrub bottoms and panties lay on the floor beside the bed, along with a pile of Sean's clothes.

Sean said, "You sure you don't want a go?"

Neal said nothing.

Sean shrugged. "Suit yourself. I need a shower."

Neal said nothing, just watched Ashley who continued to sob.

"Hey," Sean said, snapping his fingers to get Neal's attention.

Neal blinked, shifted his gaze to look at him.

Sean said, "Are you sure you don't want a go? You keep looking at her like that, I can't imagine what else you want with her."

Tears brimmed Ashley's eyes, fell down her cheeks.

"I think we should leave her here," Neal said.

The smile on Sean's face fell off. "Say what?"

"When we leave, she stays here."

"Bullshit."

"The old man said we're supposed to check in with them before we leave. But we'll just leave, you and me. We'll be hours away before they find her."

"We're not leaving her here."

"You wanted a hostage, Sean, she's no longer a hostage."

"The hell she isn't. What'd you call her then?"

"A distraction."

"She ain't no distraction."

Neal held his gaze steady with Sean's, said nothing.

Sean nodded finally, looking back and forth between Neal and Ashley. "You know, I think we're all a little too tense. Let's give it an hour and see where we're at then. Let me take a shower first, and you"—Sean winked Neal—"you release your tension any way you see fit."

He headed toward the bathroom, slipping his boxer shorts off as he went, tossing them at the pile of clothes on the floor.

The door closed and a moment later the shower came on.

Neal glanced again at Ashley on the bed. She'd stopped sobbing, but tears still fell down her cheeks.

Neal watched the bathroom door as he approached the bed. The knife sat on the bedside table. He picked it up and ejected the blade and used the blade to cut Ashley's bindings and loosened the strip of towel around her head.

"Don't get too excited," he said. "I can't let you leave. But I couldn't bear to see you tied up like that anymore."

Ashley sat up on the bed. Her eyes flitted toward the panties and scrub bottoms on the floor.

"Oh, right."

Neal grabbed the bottoms and panties off the floor and handed them to her. He kept his back to Ashley while she put them back on.

When Ashley spoke, her voice was a hoarse whisper.

"Are you going to kill me?"

Neal turned back around, shook his head.

"Is *he* going to kill me?"

"I'm going to do everything in my power to make sure he doesn't."

She started trembling, her gaze shifting to the bathroom door and the hiss of the running water behind it.

Neal sat down on the edge of the bed, causing Ashley to startle and tense up.

"I'm not going to touch you," Neal whispered. He closed the knife. "I'm sorry for what he did to you, but I ..."

Her voice quivered. "You *let* him."

"I had no other choice."

"He *raped* me."

Neal looked away from her. Took a deep breath. Forced himself to look at Ashley again as he whispered, "Everything will be okay."

Her eyes grew intense. "Everything will *not* be okay."

"Shh," Neal said, glancing again at the bathroom door.

"Don't tell me to be quiet." Her voice rising in pitch. "He's a monster. *You're* a monster. You're both monsters."

Another glance at the bathroom door. "Keep your voice down."

Ashley sucked in air to scream.

Neal lurched forward. He clamped a hand over her mouth.

Ashley's wide eyes stared back at him.

"Don't scream," Neal whispered. "If you want to stay alive, don't scream."

The intensity in her eyes didn't change, but her body seemed to deflate.

"If I release my hand, do you promise not to scream?"

She didn't answer at first, just stared back at Neal. Then, finally, she nodded.

"I'm not kidding. If you scream, there's a good chance he'll kill you. I will do whatever I can to stop him, but it won't be easy. Do you understand?"

She nodded again.

Neal leaned back, taking his hand away from Ashley's mouth.

She squinted at him. "You don't act like a criminal."

He stared at her for a long moment. Glanced again at the bathroom door. "That's because I'm not."

Her frown deepened. "What does that mean?"

Another glance at the bathroom door. Neal opened his mouth, hesitated, then whispered, "Everything will be okay."

"I don't believe you. If you're not a criminal, then what are you?"

Another hesitation. "I'm an FBI agent."

For a second Ashley said nothing. Then she rolled her eyes, shook her head. "Give me a break."

"It's true. Sean Wescott stole something from the FBI. I was sent in undercover to break him out of prison and retrieve that something."

"You're lying."

Neal sat back. "I don't know what you want me to say, how I should prove it to you, but it's true."

"I don't believe you."

"That's fine. But it still doesn't mean it's not true."

"Is Neal Palmer even your real name?"

He shook his head. "My real name is Logan Taylor."

She watched him, studying his face, then shook her head again. "If you're not lying, where are the other FBI agents?"

"They're out there. I just need to call them." He shook his head then as if to clear it. "Shit."

He rose from the bed, turned to the phone on the bedside table.

"You're going to call them now?" Ashley asked.

He glanced again at the bathroom door. "I wasn't going to, but now that you know I might as well. I couldn't call earlier."

As he reached for the phone, the shower in the bathroom stopped.

Ashley whispered, "Now what?"

He said nothing, his hand hovering inches above the receiver.

Ashley asked, "How many FBI agents are there?"

For the very first time, he frowned at her.

Just as the bathroom door opened and Sean stepped out, wrapped in a towel, using a hand towel to dry his head. He noticed first that Ashley was no longer tied to the bed, then noticed Neal—Logan Taylor?—with his hand right above the phone, his other hand still gripping the switchblade.

Sean cleared his throat, dropping the hand towel to the floor.

"Now just what the holy hell is going on here?"

17

Henry's cell phone vibrated in his pocket. He pulled it out, checked the screen, and flipped open the phone saying, "Hello, Lewis."

"How are things going?"

"Not so good. It appears Wescott and Palmer killed a gas station clerk and abducted a woman."

"I haven't seen anything on the news."

"They're going to announce it soon, I believe. At least, they are about the gas station clerk. They're holding off saying anything about the woman until they know her identity."

"Jesus Christ." Lewis took a deep breath. "Where are you now?"

"Still with Lieutenant Marsh. We decided it best to keep moving. Wescott and Palmer were headed north, from what we can tell, so we're on the highway. How are things back there?"

"Some people have been asking where you went."

"Like who?"

"The FBI agents you spoke to earlier for one. The governor for two."

"Well," Henry said, "the governor will have to wait another day to fire me. Thanks for checking in, Lewis. If anything else comes up, I'll let you know."

Henry closed the phone and just sat there in the passenger seat of the police cruiser, watching the landscape zip past. They'd been on the road for a half hour now, neither one of them speaking.

"My correctional captain checking in," Henry said.

Lieutenant Marsh nodded, his focus on the highway. "What's that about the governor firing you?"

"I figure after what happened, the state will have no choice but to let me go. Either I'll be forced into early retirement or they'll fire me."

"But it's not like it was your fault."

"When you're the warden of a prison," Henry said, "everything that goes wrong is your fault. Tell me, Lieutenant Marsh, are you a religious man?"

"I used to go to church when I was a kid. Then when I was married, we'd take the kids every Christmas and Easter."

"You're not married anymore?"

Lieutenant Marsh shook his head. "Been divorced four years now. Barely see my kids anymore. Their new stepdad spoils them rotten. Fact is, I wasn't a good father. Looking back at it, I don't think I ever really tried. Why'd you ask about me being a religious man?"

Henry stared out his window. "I've been a practicing Catholic all my life. I'm used to asking God for forgiveness. But after this"—he shook his head—"I don't even know where to start."

"What do you mean?"

"Do I ask God for forgiveness for me allowing Palmer and Wescott to escape? What they may have done to Maryann Webster? For what they did to that gas station clerk, and what they may now be doing to this woman?"

"I may not be a religious man, but I don't see how you can be responsible for any of that. It's not as if you *allowed* them to escape in the first place."

"Again, I'm the warden of the prison. I oversee everything. Had I paid better attention, been more on top of my correctional officers, maybe Palmer and Wescott would never have managed to escape. Maybe Maryann and that clerk would still be alive. Maybe that young woman would be home with her family."

"I think you're being too hard on yourself."

"Maybe," Henry said. "Then again, maybe not."

The phone vibrated in his hand. On the screen was an unfamiliar number. Henry answered it, listened for a moment, and said, "Sergeant Baker, before you continue, let me put you on speakerphone so that Lieutenant Marsh can hear." Once Henry hit the speakerphone button, he said, "Go ahead, Sergeant."

Sergeant Baker said, "Yes, well, the reason I'm calling is you asked to be updated on any new developments."

"That's right. Have you identified the woman yet?"

"Not quite."

"What does that mean?"

"We finally managed to get a good shot of the car's license plate from a highway cam several miles away from the gas station. From what we could tell, both men were in the car with the woman. The car's a navy blue Mazda 6 sedan. We ran the license plate and the car's registered to a Hayley Adams."

"Has her family been notified yet? When do you plan to announce it to the press?"

"Well, here's the thing. The car was reported stolen this morning."

Henry frowned. "Who reported it stolen?"

"Hayley Adams."

"So ... the woman from the gas station—"

"Is not Hayley Adams," Sergeant Baker said. "That's all we

know right now. We're still going to make a press release about the new information. An APB is already out regarding the Mazda. As for who the woman from the gas station is, we have no idea."

18

Sean waited several long seconds for an answer, and when none was given, he said, "Well? What's going on here?"

Neal said nothing. Neither did Ashley, who was no longer gagged.

"Why is she untied?"

Neal stepped back from the bedside table. Glanced down at Ashley, then said to Sean, "I thought she needed a break."

"You thought."

"That's right. Just like I think we're through with her. When we leave, she stays. We'll tie her to the bed like I said earlier. The cleaning lady will find her."

"Really," Sean said. He flicked his eyes to Ashley. "And what do you have to say for yourself?"

Ashley said nothing at first, just sat completely still, a statue. Then she leaned forward, rising from the bed, and started to approach Sean. There was something different about the way she held her body now. It appeared looser, not such a bundle of nerves. Like she was suddenly comfortable in this surrounding. Like she suddenly had no fear.

"What do I have to say for myself?" she said, stepping up close to Sean, her face tilted toward his so their noses were only inches apart. "I say he's a fed."

Ashley's bag still sat on the TV stand. Without a word, Sean stepped past Ashley, dipped his hand into the bag and brought back out a compact Colt .45, aimed it straight at Neal.

"Surprised?"

Neal ejected the switchblade at his side.

Sean said, "Really? You think that knife is going to stop you from a bullet?"

Neal said nothing.

Ashley had turned, was leaning against the wall, her arms crossed. "His name isn't Neal Palmer. It's Logan Taylor."

"Logan Taylor," Sean said, taking his time to repeat the name. "Gotta say, part of me thinks Neal Palmer is a better name."

Neal kept the switchblade held down at his side. Didn't say a word.

Sean smiled. "Of course, there's the chance you may not actually be an FBI agent after all. That for some reason you told poor little Ashley that to, what, try to cheer her up? Give her some hope? Yeah, there's certainly a chance that may be the case, but I don't buy it."

Logan said, "A team of FBI agents are outside right this moment. They've been tailing us ever since we left the prison. Do yourself a favor and drop the weapon."

Sean laughed, the Colt in his hand not wavering an inch. "Good one. But if a team was trailing us ever since Wrightsville, they would have intervened at the gas station." Sean paused, studying Logan's face. "Then again, maybe they wouldn't have. Not if Agent Ramirez wants what I have so badly."

Logan made no reaction. Just stood there, the switchblade held tightly at his side.

"I'll be honest with you," Sean said. "I was kinda hoping you were legit. I mean, I like you. Or I liked whatever character you made yourself. We got along, didn't we? Shared stories, told jokes. I knew I could never let my guard down around anybody, but I got close with you."

"Let me guess," Logan said. "Now you're going to feel even worse having to kill me."

"Something like that. See, I always knew Agent Ramirez would have something up her sleeve. I figured she'd try to get to me while I was inside. That's why I was extra vigilant around new people after I arrived at Wrightsville. I'd been in Albany six months and thought it was weird why they wanted to transfer me. And you"—Sean grinned—"you'd already been there three months. So yeah, I thought that was suspect. But then I did my research. I knew about your arrest record and how you'd spent some time down south. After that, there wasn't much else, but it seemed real enough. I'm guessing Agent Ramirez pulled out all the stops to make sure her little lapdog fit in just right."

Sean shook his head, smiling.

"And me, well, I'm guessing you know all there is to know about me. Or at least all Agent Ramirez *wants* you to know. Let me guess. She gave you a thick file with my name on it, told you to memorize everything. Did you do any other research? Did you look for anything outside that file?"

Logan said nothing.

"You probably didn't even know about Ashley. Pretty much *nobody* knew about Ashley, which is why we knew she could use her real name and no fed would even blink. We figured out a way to communicate before I went in. So once you filled me in on your plan to escape, I was already bringing her up to speed."

Sean motioned with the Colt toward the chair in the corner.

"Why don't you have a seat?"

"I'll stand, thank you."

"Suit yourself." Sean laughed again. "I'll tell you, you did a great job. I could tell something was going on with you for a while. You were just so ... quiet, so guarded. But not too guarded, if that makes sense. You made it so that I noticed something was off and forced *me* to try to figure out what was going on. It was brilliant. I mean, no way could you have brought the fact that you were escaping straight to me. That would have raised too many red flags. In fact, you seemed pissed when I was first assigned as your cellmate. Wouldn't talk to me for weeks. So making it so that *I* was the one who stumbled on it, who found out what you were up to—that was pure genius. Whose idea was that, by the way, yours or Agent Ramirez's? Or was it somebody else's?"

Logan said nothing.

"I can't imagine there are many others. No, Agent Ramirez would want to make this top secret. She wouldn't want a chance that her dirty laundry might get out for everybody to see."

"What dirty laundry?"

"It doesn't concern you. But what should concern you is the fact that I'm currently aiming a pistol at your face and you're holding a knife and there are not any fucking agents outside."

"Yes, there are."

"He's lying," Ashley said. "He told me as much while you were in the shower. He was just about to make a call when you stepped out."

"Maybe that's what I wanted her to think," Logan said, his gaze steady with Sean's.

Sean laughed again. "I like you. I truly do. So it's going to suck when I have to place a bullet between those baby blue eyes of yours."

Logan tilted his head toward Ashley. "She was a nice touch."

"Wasn't she, though? I needed to know just how real you were. Figured I'd see the real you once we brought an innocent into play."

"It made no sense to me why you wanted to ditch the truck. We could have taken that anywhere, been out of the state before they realized we were gone. And then we waited for over an hour until she showed up. I did think that was weird at the time. There had been other cars which had come and gone before then."

"Yes, that's because there was no way Ashley knew when we would make it to that gas station. In fact, all she knew was that we would be at *a* gas station along the highway that night. Ashley, how many gas stations did you stop at before we met up?"

"Five," she said. "Bought the same water and pretzels at each one."

"So no child," Logan said.

Ashley shook her head.

"Then why the baby toy?"

"It was there when I stole the car. Thought it was a nice touch. Made up a name for my kid on the drive, a whole back story." She grinned at Sean. "Impressed?"

"You always impress me, baby." Sean said to Logan, "The rape was the ultimate test. Had you passed that one, I decided it was time to trust you."

"You mean if I wanted sloppy seconds?"

"Had you wanted sloppy seconds, I would have come up with a reason why you couldn't. Fact is, me and Ashley haven't been together for two years. It was nice. Wasn't it, baby?"

"Sure was."

Logan said, "Are we done?"

"I believe we are. I just felt that you deserved to know. Like I said, I thought of you as a friend. I knew I couldn't ever trust you completely, but I wanted to. Fact is, I would have given you the money."

"That's a shame."

"What would you have done with it, anyway? I know when we talked before you said you would buy a boat, sail down the coast, spend the rest of your life in the Caribbean. Honestly, I'm not sure if you could get by the rest of your life on just a half million dollars after buying that boat, but it was a nice thought. Tell me, was that really what you would do or was that just part of your bullshit cover?"

"Give me the money and maybe we'll find out."

Sean's hand tightened on the Colt's grip. "I never wanted to be an informant. I never wanted to end up in Wrightsville. I never wanted any of this shit to happen. I don't think Agent Ramirez ever told you the full story, did she?"

Logan didn't answer.

"Oh well. I'll let you decide. How do you want it? Just make it fast, one to the head?"

Logan said nothing, his fingers tight around the switchblade.

"I know your instinct is to fight," Sean said, "but don't waste your time. I want to, I'll just shoot you in the stomach, let you bleed out. It'll be painful. Is that what you want?"

"Seems fitting enough," Logan said. "That's how you killed Agent Weber."

Sean sighed, shaking his head. "I didn't kill him. I shot him, yes, but that's because he tried to attack me."

"You're lying. You killed him, you took the money, and then you stole the laptop."

"What the hell are you talking about?"

Before Logan could respond, a voice boomed on a bullhorn outside.

"*Sean Wescott and Neal Palmer! We know you're in there! Come out with your hands up!*"

Logan smiled at Sean. "I told you there were agents outside."

19

Keeping the Colt and his gaze leveled at Logan, Sean moved across the motel room to the door. He stepped up close to the door and broke his gaze with Logan to glance out through the peephole. A second, that was all it took, and then he leaned back and maintained his stare on Logan.

"Yep, those are FBI agents," Sean said. "If the FBI's now hiring redneck teenagers to do their dirty work for them."

Logan shrugged. "It was worth a shot."

Outside, the voice boomed over the bullhorn again.

"*Sean Wescott and Neal Palmer! We know you're in there! Come out with your hands up!*"

Ashley asked Sean, "What are we going to do?"

Sean said nothing for a moment, watching Logan. "Maybe we should send you out there. Those kids look like they might have itchy trigger fingers. They catch a glimpse of you, they're apt to blow your head off."

Logan said, "You do realize you're still wearing a fucking towel, don't you?"

Before Sean could respond, Logan lurched forward. Not toward Sean and the gun and the door leading outside, but toward the bathroom.

Ashley jumped, startled, and tried to grab for Logan, but he breezed past her without any trouble.

Sean tracked him with the Colt but didn't pull the trigger, watching as Logan disappeared into the bathroom and slammed the door shut.

Ashley said, "Why didn't you shoot him?"

"Didn't want to spook the rednecks outside."

Sean hurried over to the bathroom. He tried the knob but it was locked. He slammed his fist against the door, stood back to kick it in, but Ashley placed a hand on his arm.

"What about them?" she asked, gesturing at the motel room door.

Outside, the redneck with the bullhorn again: "*Sean Wescott and Neal Palmer! Don't make us tell you again!*"

Sean paused, breathing heavy, trying to think. He looked toward the motel door, then at the pile of his clothes on the floor, then down at the Colt in his hand, before he looked back up at Ashley.

"I have an idea."

20

Brett lowered the bullhorn and looked at Ryan standing beside him. "You sure they're in there?"

Ryan nodded. "Positive. Nobody's come or gone since I saw the one entering twenty minutes ago."

George said, "Maybe they're discussing their surrender."

Ryan grinned. "If they know what's best for them, those two will hurry out with their tails between their legs."

The three of them stood in the parking lot forty yards away from Room 9, two oversized Dodge Rams flanking them. One was Brett's, the other was Blake's, who had headed around the end of the building to keep an eye on the bathroom window in case the two escapees got it into their heads that they could slip out the back.

"Do it again," Ryan said.

Brett looked down at the bullhorn in his hand. In his other hand, he gripped a Glock 19. Strapped over his shoulder was an AR-15. Ryan and George had similar AR-15s strapped over their shoulders, as did Blake back behind the motel. Each rifle fully loaded, with an extra magazine just in case. Which hopefully they would not need, but these were violent criminals, murderers, men who had escaped a maximum-security prison, so they weren't taking any chances.

"Hey," Ryan said to Brett. "Do it again."

Brett said, "How positive are you those are the guys?"

"I said I was positive."

"Maybe they're just two faggots on their honeymoon or something."

Ryan reached out and grabbed the bullhorn from Brett. He held it to his mouth.

"*Hey, you two assholes in there better come out in the next five seconds or it ain't gonna be pretty!*"

George sniggered. He had his AR-15 raised, the stock against his shoulder, his eye lined up with the sight aimed straight at the door.

Ryan said, "*Five!*"

Nothing.

"*Four!*"

Still nothing.

"*Three!*"

The door opened. Not entirely, just a couple inches.

George's finger touched the rifle's trigger as Brett aimed his Glock, and Ryan, fumbling, dropped the bullhorn to grab his own rifle.

A man yelled from inside Room 9, "We have a hostage!"

The three teenagers shot each other quick, uncertain looks.

Ryan shouted, "Who do you have?"

"A woman!"

"Prove it!"

For a long moment nothing happened, and then the door opened even wider and a woman leaned out. She was young, in her early thirties, short dark hair. She looked terrified.

"Please," she sobbed, "don't let them—"

She screamed as she was yanked back into the room.

Brett kept his aim on the open motel room door when he whispered, "Maybe we should call the police."

Ryan shouted, "You need to let her go!"

Silence.

Brett whispered, "I don't like this."

"Shut up," Ryan whispered back. Then shouted, "Hey, ass-holes! Did you hear what I said?"

From inside the room, the man's voice shouted back, "If we let her go, what do we get in return?"

Ryan didn't hesitate. He shouted, "We won't kill you!"

More silence. It lasted maybe ten seconds before the man shouted again.

"I don't believe you!"

Ryan shouted, "You let her go first, then come out with your hands up, and we'll make sure the police take you back to prison! Nobody's gotta get hurt!"

Brett whispered again, "I don't like this."

Ryan said nothing. He kept his aim straight at the open door.

"Okay!" the man inside Room 9 shouted. "We're letting her go!"

The woman reappeared a moment later. She stepped out of the room slowly at first, looking back inside as if a weapon was aimed at her. Then she was on the walkway and glanced up and saw the three teenagers with their weapons trained on her and froze.

Ryan said, "It's okay. We're here to help. Come on, hurry!"

She didn't move. Just stood there, as if stunned. She said, her voice trembling, "There—there—there are only three of you?"

"And one around back," Ryan said. "Come on!"

Ashley hurried forward. The three teenagers stayed motion-less, keeping their weapons aimed at Room 9, until she reached them. She started crying, tears in her eyes, her entire body shaking violently.

"Oh God, oh God, oh God!" she sobbed.

"It's okay," Ryan said. "Stay behind us." He shouted at the motel room, "Okay, time for you two guys to come out with your hands up!"

Nothing happened. Several long seconds passed with no answer. In fact, it was completely silent. Even the girl had stopped sobbing.

Ryan glanced back to check on her, and that was when she punched him in the face. He stumbled back, stepped on the bullhorn, twisted his ankle, and fell to the ground. His rifle fell with him too, clattering to the pavement.

At that same moment, Sean stepped out of Room 9. He fired the Colt several times, first at Brett, then at George. Not a skilled marksman by any account, his shots were steady but wide. One of them hit Brett in his left arm. Another hit George in his kneecap. That was it. Still, enough to put one of the boys down momentarily and give Ashley enough time to grab the rifle Ryan had dropped and bring it up and, at such close range, fire straight into Ryan's chest. Then she turned and fired into Brett's chest. By that point, Sean had advanced across the parking lot, placed the muzzle to George's head, and pulled the trigger.

Blake, who'd heard the gunfire, had abandoned his post behind the motel and hurried around to the parking lot. Seeing what had become of his friends, he fired at Sean and Ashley who dove for cover behind one of the pickup trucks. Blake rushed forward, and as he neared, Sean circled the pickup and stepped up behind Blake and fired two rounds into Blake's back.

"You okay?" Sean asked Ashley.

She looked down at herself as if to make sure, then nodded.

"Check one of the pickups for a key," he said, heading back toward Room 9.

"Where are you going?"

"To finish what I started."

"We need to leave!"

"Just get the pickup ready!" he shouted, stepping up onto the walkway and entering the room, the Colt aimed, in case Logan had slipped out of the bathroom during the shootout and was right now hiding behind the door.

The room was vacant. The bathroom door still closed.

Sean kicked at the door once, twice, three times. On the fourth kick, the door finally gave way and swung inward. He stepped in, the Colt raised, but the bathroom was empty. The window open, the screen pushed out from where Logan must have climbed through.

Out in the parking lot, Ashley leaned on one of the pickup's horns.

Sean grabbed her purse off the TV stand and hurried back outside. He paused by one of the teenagers wearing a cowboy hat. He grabbed the hat, the kid's Glock 19 and AR-15 and extra magazines, and opened the driver's door and told Ashley to move over.

As she climbed into the passenger seat, Ashley asked, "Logan?"

"Slipped out the back."

"He'll contact the FBI."

"Yes, but by that point we'll be long gone," Sean said, putting the Dodge Ram in drive, stomping on the gas, and whipping them out of the parking lot onto the main road.

21

Logan rounded the corner at the end of the motel just as the Dodge Ram screeched out of the parking lot.

He hesitated a moment, taking in the scene, the dead bodies splayed out on the pavement.

The Ram was a dot in the distance now.

Logan hurried forward. He surveyed the four bodies on the ground. All of them were dead. He stood over Ryan, shaking his head.

"Should have let me use the phone," he muttered.

One of the motel room doors opened. An old man poked his head out.

"Is it over?" he shouted.

Logan said, "Call the police."

"I already did!"

"Then stay in your room until they arrive."

The old man took a courageous step out onto the walkway. "Who the hell put you in charge?"

Logan grabbed one of the AR-15s off the ground and aimed

it at the old man. "Get back in your goddamned room and lock the door!"

The old man disappeared inside, the door slamming shut behind him.

Ryan lay on his stomach, so the bulge at the back of his waist was noticeable.

Logan crouched down, set the rifle aside, and flipped up Ryan's shirt to reveal the Glock he'd secured there. He wiggled it free, dropped the mag, found it fully loaded, and then stood, reinserting the mag and pulling the slide.

He stuffed the Glock in the back of his own pants as he searched Ryan for his cell phone. It was in the kid's front jeans pocket, but he needed a four-digit passcode to access it.

Logan checked the three other teenagers' pockets. Each of them had cell phones, but only one of them didn't require a passcode to unlock the screen. This was a cheap Samsung with a broken screen. It had forty percent battery power left.

He checked the Dodge Ram next. The keys were in the ignition.

Logan stepped up inside, noticing the curtains moving from the room where the old man was hiding. The old man now peered out at him. Logan shut the pickup's door, started the engine, and threw the gearshift into reverse.

He was on the main road ten seconds later. Sean and Ashley had taken off, what, two minutes ago? Assuming they were doing over sixty miles per hour, that put them already two miles ahead of Logan.

Logan pressed down on the gas pedal. The Ram's engine roared. The needle ticked up and up. Keeping one hand on the wheel, he dug the broken Samsung from his pocket and pulled up the phone application. Dialed a number he'd memorized two years ago and put the phone to his ear, murmuring, "Come on, come on, come on," as it rang and rang. Finally, a voice mail picked up. Nothing personal, just a robotic voice telling the caller to leave a message.

Beep.

"Wescott was on to me from the start. The girl we abducted turned out to be his girlfriend. Her name is Ashley Gilmore. They just left the Green Valley Inn where Sean and Ashley murdered four kids. I managed to escape and am following them now. They're at least two minutes ahead of me in a red Dodge Ram headed west. I have no idea when you'll get this message, but call when you can. I don't know the number of this phone—I took it off one of the dead kids—so hopefully you can trace it."

Logan disconnected the phone. He made sure it was switched to ring instead of vibrate for incoming calls. He tossed the phone on the passenger seat, put both hands on the wheel, and forced the Ram up to eighty, eighty-five, ninety.

22

The road curved and twisted, Logan doing his best to tap the brake as little as possible, keeping the needle above sixty miles per hour, trees and houses whipping past on both sides of the road, any of those places Sean may have parked the pickup to hide.

But then, after several minutes, the road came to an end.

Logan applied pressure to the brakes, eased to a stop. A state highway sat perpendicular. North and south. Left or right.

His fingers squeezed the steering wheel tightly, so tightly his arms began to shake, and with a shout of frustration he smacked the steering wheel with his fist.

The cell phone on the passenger seat rang.

Logan picked it up. No number on the screen, just the words INCOMING CALL.

He pressed the green answer button, placed the phone to his ear. Didn't say anything. On the other end there was silence, but it was an energized silence, someone clearly there wanting to speak or shout or scream.

Finally, a female voice said, "Logan?"

He released a heavy breath. "It's me."

Agent Gloria Ramirez said, "My God. Are you okay?"

"For now."

"Any luck with Wescott?"

"None. The road came to a highway. I have no idea where they went, assuming they didn't get off the road earlier. Where are you?"

"About an hour out. We're headed to you now."

"Do you have access to traffic cams?"

There was a slight hesitation. "Yes and no."

"What does that mean?"

"It means we do but it will take time to backtrack to your location."

Logan smacked the steering wheel with his fist again.

On the highway, vehicles passed back and forth, some going north, others going south.

Gloria said, "What does your gut tell you?"

Logan was quiet for a moment, thinking about it. "Wescott kept telling me to go north. He wouldn't say where we were going, just to keep going north."

"And?"

"And I'm not sure if that's important. Either he actually did want us to head north, or he had us head north because he was playing with me, waiting to see if I would pass his test. Gloria, I'm sorry I fucked up."

"You didn't fuck up."

"He figured me out."

"Don't beat yourself up over it."

Logan shook his head, watching the traffic passing back and forth. "Fuck it. I'm heading south."

"Are you sure?"

He hesitated. "No."

"This is important, Logan."

"No shit it's important. I just—fuck!"

He smacked the wheel a third time, then slammed on the gas and jerked the wheel taking the Ram north.

Gloria said, "What did you decide?"

"North."

She was quiet for a moment. "We're accessing the traffic cams in the meantime. If you have any luck, call the number again."

"What's your cell number?"

"It's best if my number doesn't show up on the kid's phone. Just call the automated number. It'll alert me as soon as you leave a voice mail. And, Logan?"

The Ram's engine roared, its needle rising and rising, Logan swerving from lane to lane to bypass the slower moving vehicles.

"Yeah."

"It's good to hear your voice."

"Thanks. It's good to hear your voice too."

"I'll see you soon."

Before Logan could respond, the phone went dead in his ear. He tossed it on the passenger seat, grabbed the steering wheel with both hands again, and floored the gas, surveying the distance for any sign of Wescott.

23

After several miles, Logan let up on the gas, letting the needle drop back down to a safe seventy miles per hour. The last thing he needed was to get pulled over by a cop.

But as he drove, the Dodge Ram's grill eating up the highway, Logan found his foot on the gas growing heavier and heavier, the needle rising again, until he was doing ninety. He kept his focus on the distance, on the places where cops might be set up for a speed trap, on the vehicles in front and behind him, trying to spot if any were undercover cops cruising the highway for hapless speeders.

If he maintained ninety miles per hour and Wescott maintained at most seventy-five miles per hour, Logan had a better shot at catching up with him.

Assuming Wescott hadn't headed south in the first place.

Assuming too the man hadn't pulled off the highway at any of the exits. Only two had gone by so far, and Logan had whipped past them without a second's hesitation, which in retrospect may not have been wise.

It was another ten minutes, swerving from lane to lane, constantly checking the rearview and side mirrors, the needle steady at ninety miles per hour, that he spotted a Dodge Ram farther ahead.

At least, the overlarge pickup *looked* like a Dodge Ram from this distance.

Logan let up on the gas, let the needle dip back down to seventy-five. If he came up on the pickup too quickly, there was a chance Wescott—if the driver truly was Wescott—would notice him.

He stayed in the right lane, straining to spot anything on the pickup that might confirm its passengers.

The Dodge Ram was a half mile away, then a quarter of a mile away.

Not wanting to get any closer, Logan hit the cruise control and grabbed the cell phone off the passenger seat. The battery was now at twenty-five percent. He made a quick survey of the pickup's cab for a charger but didn't see one. He leaned over, opened the glove box, rifled through the junk in there but didn't come up with anything useful.

He redialed the number and waited for the voice mail to pick up, said, "Call me," then clicked off.

The phone rang a minute later.

Gloria said, "Status?"

"I believe I have them."

"Seriously?"

"Yes. They're on the highway headed north. I'm a quarter of a mile back, trying to maintain the distance."

"So you're not positive."

"I only caught a glimpse of the pickup as it was leaving the parking lot. It was a large, red Dodge Ram. That's what's in front of me now. Granted, there's the chance this is a different large red Dodge Ram, but my gut tells me otherwise."

"Can't you get any closer?"

"Not without being spotted. Even now I'm worried I might

be too close. It's impossible to say how observant Wescott actually is. I could ride up on his ass and he might not even notice, but I don't want to take the chance."

"I agree."

"Where are you now?"

"Still an hour out. We finally got access to the traffic cams."

"The phone I'm using is going to die soon. I don't have a charger."

"Then hopefully we'll catch up with you before that happens. How are you on gas?"

Logan checked the gauge. "I'm at a half tank."

"Good. Stay with Wescott and call if anything changes."

She clicked off without another word.

Logan tossed the cell phone on the passenger seat again. He then realized for the first time that he still had on the fake glasses and tossed them on the seat too. He leaned his head back on the headrest, his hand on the wheel, his gaze on the pickup a quarter mile away that may or may not contain Sean Wescott and Ashley Gilmore.

24

The Green Valley Inn's parking lot was a circus by the time they arrived at just after twelve o'clock. Nearly six police vehicles—local and state—as well as three ambulances. Two news crews had shown up too, each van proudly announcing its station's identification, but they had been regulated to a spot on the other side of the office, which gave them hardly any view of the crime scene.

At first one of the cops working the perimeter wouldn't let them in. Said that they already had too many police on scene. But when Henry made it known who he was, the cop's attitude changed. An almost embarrassed look crossed the cop's face, though it was difficult to say who the look was meant for, the cop or Henry.

"Go ahead," the cop said, waving them through.

Lieutenant Marsh parked the cruiser and they got out, taking in the crisp cold air.

Another cop approached them. "Help you?"

"This is Warden Henry Barnes," Lieutenant Marsh said by way of introduction. "I brought him up from Wrightsville. We've been tracking the two escapees."

The cop studied Henry for a moment as if he wasn't sure whether to believe this was the man who had overseen Wescott and Palmer.

"Not much for you to do here now," the cop said. "Those two are long gone."

"How long ago?"

"The 911 call came in over an hour ago. Three units responded, but it took them nearly ten minutes before they arrived. We're out in the boondocks, after all. As you can see"—he motioned at the frenzy of police behind him—"we have it pretty well covered."

Henry said, "May we ask what happened?"

The cop did that thing again where he studied Henry's face for a moment before sighing. "The two were holed up here."

"Were they by themselves?" Lieutenant Marsh asked.

"No, that's the strange thing. They had a woman with them. Only ... well, we got just one witness account so far, and we're not even sure how much of it we should believe."

Henry frowned. "What do you mean?"

"Our witness isn't necessarily the most reliable person in town. He's got some sexual assault charges on his record, some disorderly conduct. Not to mention he reeked of liquor when he gave his statement."

Lieutenant Marsh said, "What did he say?"

"Said those dead boys called for your escapees to give themselves up. One of the escapees said they had a hostage. The boys told them to send out the hostage. So they did. This woman came running out and hid behind the boys. That's when she punched one of the boys and took his rifle."

Henry shook his head as if to clear it. "Can you say that again?"

The cop grinned. "See, I told you he's not the most reliable witness."

"You're saying the witness claims the woman helped Wescott and Palmer?"

"That's not even the strangest part. He said that after the woman and one of your escapees had killed the kids, they took off in one of the pickups."

"What about the other convict?" Lieutenant Marsh said.

"Yeah, about him. The witness said it looked like he was chasing after them."

Henry frowned again. "What do you mean?"

"The other escapee ran up just after the pickup took off. That's when the witness decided to step out of his room. The other escapee told him to call the police. When our witness said he had, the escapee told him to go back inside and lock the door. When our witness questioned this, the escapee grabbed one of the rifles and aimed it at him."

There was a brief silence, both men processing this.

"Let me get this straight," Henry said. "One of the escapees *told* the witness to call the police?"

The cop was nodding. "That's right."

"But that ... that doesn't make any sense."

"Tell me about it. The room was rented this morning around six thirty. They paid cash, gave some bullshit name. The old man who worked the desk last night said he remembered a young couple rented the room."

"A young couple," Henry echoed.

"Yes, a man and a woman. The old man didn't remember the woman saying much at all. I mean, we've been telling people to be on the lookout for two dangerous criminals. Not a couple, for Christ's sake."

Henry said, "And the woman, if your witness is to be believed, killed some of those boys over there."

"That's right," the cop said.

Lieutenant Marsh turned away from them, slipping his cell

phone from his pocket. He placed it to his ear, listened for several seconds, said he understood, and then stuffed the phone back into his pocket.

"What is it?" Henry asked.

Lieutenant Marsh thanked the cop for his time. He said, "I need to head out. Warden Barnes, I'm afraid you're going to have to stay here."

"What's happened?"

"Just got a call from my commander. There's been a sighting of what we believe is one of them. It's best if you stay here."

"Why?"

Lieutenant Marsh hesitated again. "I shouldn't have even brought you along in the first place. It was stupid of me, and I don't want to put you at any further risk."

"You mean you want to cover your ass."

"It's not just that. After what these two have done, we're not taking any chances."

Henry glanced around as he whispered, "You plan to kill them."

"Not necessarily. If there's an opening to take them out, that's what we're going to do. It may not be legal, which is why my commander doesn't want you along."

Henry almost laughed. "Do you think I care if these two die? No, I'm coming with you."

Lieutenant Marsh was quiet for a long moment, looking past Henry at the crime scene and the news crews set up on the other side of the office.

"It'd be better if you stayed here," he said.

"I understand," Henry said, "but I need to come. I need to be involved. You understand why, don't you? I need to do penance any way I can."

25

Logan stayed with the pickup. Sometimes he dropped back to let a car get in front of him, and sometimes he sped up to pass another car, as staying in one lane and maintaining the same speed might become too noticeable.

A half hour passed, then an hour. Logan saw flashing lights in the distance at one point and expected it to be a roadblock. But it just turned out to be a state police trooper who had pulled over a tractor-trailer.

The Dodge Ram ahead of Logan moved over to the left lane just as did the rest of the traffic passing the cop and then moved back to the right lane. Sean never even tapped the brakes.

The cell phone didn't ring. It did beep once, though, a text from the kid's mom.

WHERE ARE U?

Logan didn't answer. He noted the battery life was at eighteen percent and tossed the phone on the passenger seat.

Fifteen minutes later the phone rang. Logan almost answered it without looking at the screen. Instead of INCOMING CALL, it said MOM.

He set the phone aside. Let it keep ringing. A minute later, the phone beeped with a voice mail, the kid's mom no doubt frustrated that her son wasn't answering her.

Logan kept his focus on the pickup a quarter mile ahead of him.

The highway curved, heading east, and then curved back toward west.

After another half hour, the pickup's turn signal blinked on as it moved into the exit lane.

Logan clicked off the cruise control, let the Ram drop back even more. The hope was another vehicle or two would use the exit as well. There were currently five vehicles between Logan and the other Dodge Ram.

As it turned out, three vehicles got off at the exit.

Logan had tracked the Dodge Ram the moment it reached the overpass exit. He had watched as it waited at the stop sign and then made a right.

The Dodge Ram hadn't gotten very far. The traffic just off the highway was congested. At first this didn't make sense until Logan had exited the highway and came up the ramp and saw what lay a half mile away.

A mall.

The Black River Mall, to be exact, a massive complex of what looked to house over one hundred stores and shops, chain restaurants dotting the landscape around the enormous structure like sentinels.

The parking lot was packed at almost three o'clock in the afternoon. Today was Black Friday, the busiest shopping day of the year in the United States. That was why traffic was so congested. Everyone was headed to the mall. Including Sean Wescott and Ashley Gilmore? No, that wouldn't make sense. There was no reason for them to go to a mall. Sean's face was all over the news. He wouldn't want to be seen in such a public place.

And yet, as the Dodge Ram ahead of Logan crawled through traffic, it eventually merged over to the left turning lane.

Logan stayed back, but he couldn't stay too far back. Before, he'd tried to maintain a quarter-mile buffer between him and the other Dodge Ram, but now there were less than three hundred yards between them.

Which became a problem at the intersection, as the green arrow in the turning lane lasted no more than fifteen seconds. The Dodge Ram ahead of him went through the intersection and disappeared behind an Olive Garden.

Logan's fingers tightened around the steering wheel. He muttered, "Come on, come on, come on," watching the slow cycle of the traffic lights until the turning lane got the green arrow again.

The traffic ahead of Logan didn't seem to be in any rush. They took their time, so much so that the green arrow had turned red by the time Logan made it to the intersection.

He pulled through anyway, just as traffic in the opposing lane had gotten the go ahead to move forward.

Logan slammed on the gas, the pickup's engine roaring as he tore through the intersection, one of the cars in the other lane blaring its horn at him.

His eyes darted everywhere for the pickup. It was large and red, so it shouldn't be too difficult to spot, but there were over a thousand vehicles parked around the mall.

It also didn't help that traffic was moving even slower now closer to the mall, everyone trying to find a parking spot.

How many minutes had passed since Logan lost sight of the Dodge Ram? Had Sean Wescott known he was there this entire time, had stopped at that exit to try to lose Logan in a crush of cars? No, that didn't sound right. But still, Sean had pulled into this parking lot for a reason. If it wasn't to lose Logan, then why?

Logan spotted the large red Dodge Ram—or, at least, *a* large red Dodge Ram. It was parked a dozen spaces back from the main entrance into Macy's. He cut the wheel hard, nearly collid-ing with a car in the opposite lane.

That car screeched to a halt, the driver waving her hands wild-ly, but Logan barely paid her any attention. He noted that the other Dodge Ram was empty. He scanned the people coming and going from the main entrance, trying to spot a couple, but there were too many.

Except—wait. There were a dozen couples, yes, but in one of those couples, the man wore a cowboy hat.

Logan's gaze was so intent on the cowboy hat that he almost ran into a car backing out of a parking space.

He noticed it at the last second, slammed on his brakes.

The driver of the car in front of him glared at him for a mo-ment, then backed out and started away.

Logan swooped into the parking spot. He killed the Ram's engine, grabbed the phone and Glock off the passenger seat. He stepped out of the truck, inconspicuously tucking the Glock in the waistband of his jeans, making sure his shirt hid the weap-on from sight. There would be a bulge for anyone looking close enough, but hopefully it wouldn't get to that point.

The cowboy hat had disappeared inside.

Logan went to shut the pickup's door but paused. He leaned back inside, dug around the mess in the back of the cab, and came away with a black NASCAR cap with the number 88 on the front.

Fitting the cap on his head, Logan hurried toward the Macy's entrance, being careful not to redial the last missed call on the Samsung, which was the dead kid's mother, but the number for Agent Ramirez.

He waited for the voice mail to pick up and then the beep.

"I tracked them to the Black River Mall. Call me back as soon as possible."

He disconnected, noting the battery was now at twelve per-cent. He switched the phone back to vibrate, stuffed it in his pocket, and hurried inside.

26

Agent Gloria Ramirez called him back two minutes later.

"Did you say you tracked Wescott to a mall?"

Logan moved past the kiosks and shops, the phone to his ear, his gaze steady on the cowboy hat two hundred yards ahead of him.

The Black River Mall, as expected, was mobbed. Families and couples pushing past other families and couples, lugging shopping bags filled to the brim with Black Friday deals. Logan had seen a few other cowboy hats since he'd entered the mall, but this cowboy hat was with a brunette woman who was most certainly Ashley Gilmore.

"Yes, I have them in sight right now."

Gloria was quiet for a moment. "What is he up to now?"

"No idea. How far away are you?"

"We should be there within an hour."

"You said that an hour ago."

"Yes, and an hour ago you weren't positive you had Wescott. Now you are. We'll be there as soon as possible."

"My phone's going to die soon."

"You're at the mall. Can't you buy a charger?"

"I'd rather have as few human interactions as possible at the moment."

"Yes, of course. Again, we're on our way."

"Have you notified local authorities yet?"

Another brief silence.

"Gloria."

She sighed. "You know this is a secret operation. We can't bring in local authorities, at least not yet. What are we going to do, tell them that Wescott is at the mall? It will put everybody on high alert. The cops will be just as likely to shoot you dead as they will Wescott. Speaking of which, do you have a weapon?"

"Yes. So does he."

"Keep them in sight. Call if anything comes up. We'll be there ASAP."

She clicked off.

A soft pretzel kiosk was just ahead. Logan's stomach growled. He kept an eye on the moving cowboy hat as he purchased a pretzel and Coke.

Sean and Ashley had turned the corner up ahead. When Logan reached the corner, they were gone.

Panicked, Logan hurried forward, pushing past the families and couples, looking everywhere.

He spotted the cowboy hat moving through a candle shop.

"What the hell?" Logan whispered.

He found a bench in the middle of the corridor a few shops away and sat with his pretzel and soda. He made sure the NAS-CAR cap was low over his face, but not too conspicuous. A few teens sat on the bench adjacent, their heads bent, their gazes glued to their phones. Logan pulled the Samsung out and stared down at it too, making furtive glances toward the candle shop.

A minute passed, then another minute.

Could they have slipped out through the back storage room?

Logan sprang to his feet. He started toward the candle shop

when suddenly Sean Wescott and Ashley Gilmore appeared. Neither of them carried a bag, but they were holding hands like any happy couple.

They were headed directly toward him.

Logan turned away, trying to act as casual as possible, looking back and forth at the shops along the corridor.

He started for the record store, took two steps inside, but a clerk stocking bargain DVDs told him they didn't allow food or drink in the store.

Logan apologized and turned back around. By that point, Sean and Ashley had passed by and were headed toward the food court.

He started after them, falling in line behind a couple pushing a baby stroller. The baby was crying and the couple was arguing about what they should do with it.

Sean and Ashley didn't look like they were in any hurry. They walked slowly, hand in hand, wandering the corridor as causal shoppers without any purpose whatsoever.

None of it made any sense.

Logan carried the soda and pretzel in one hand, the cell phone in the other.

The food court was bustling. Every shop had a line. Most of the tables scattered around the middle were occupied.

Sean and Ashley went straight for an empty table. Sat down across from each other. Leaned in close, still holding hands, and kissed each other on the lips.

Just another ordinary couple in a crowd of couples.

Logan shook his head, muttered, "What the fuck is going on here?"

27

They drove north, the police cruiser going ninety, ninety-five miles per hour, swerving from one lane to the next. Lieutenant Marsh didn't use his emergency lights unless both lanes were blocked and then he flashed them, briefly, just long enough for the vehicle in their lane to move over and create a large enough pocket for them to breeze through.

They'd been on the road for forty-five minutes already, neither one of them saying much of anything, Lieutenant Marsh focused on the highway. At one point Henry's wife texted him, asking where he was, and he replied that they were following up on a lead and that he would call her later.

Then Lieutenant Marsh's cell phone beeped, and he placed it to his ear, listened a moment, said, "Okay," and pressed down on the gas even more.

"What's wrong?" Henry said.

"Nothing. It's just that we're close."

"Where?"

"We're almost there."

They took the next exit and traffic came to a standstill. A large shopping mall lay sprawled before them.

"They're in the mall?" Henry asked, incredulous.

Lieutenant Marsh only nodded, checking his blind spot as he merged over into the turning lane.

"Why don't you use your lights?"

"No lights, no sirens. We don't want to do anything that might tip them off."

Henry stared out the windshield at the mall. "It's Black Friday. There are thousands of people in there."

"Yes."

"And Palmer and Wescott are armed."

"Yes."

"Just"—Henry shook his head as if trying to clear it—"what the hell are they planning?"

Lieutenant Marsh kept his hands on the wheel, his gaze on the traffic light hanging over the intersection. "No idea. But we need to stop them before they do whatever it is they have planned."

Five minutes later they were off the main road and circling the mall parking lot.

Henry surveyed the parking lot for other police cars but didn't see any.

They came to a ramp that led down to a service entrance. A few trucks were parked around the place, as were a few mall security vehicles.

Lieutenant Marsh parked the cruiser, cut the engine.

Henry climbed out. "Where are we going?"

Lieutenant Marsh didn't answer, already headed for the service entrance.

Henry hurried to keep up.

A motion-sensored door opened as they approached. Henry followed Lieutenant Marsh inside just as a security guard was headed their way, a pack of cigarettes in his hand.

Lieutenant Marsh said, "I'm with the state police. Have you been made aware of the situation?"

The security guard frowned. "What situation?"

"Shit," Lieutenant Marsh said with a sigh. "Where's your security office?"

The guard pointed down the corridor.

"Can you show us?"

The guard looked down at the forlorn pack of cigarettes in his hand and then motioned for them to follow him.

Down at the end of the corridor was an entrance to the security office.

"Larry?" the security guard called.

Another guard poked his head out. "What's up?"

"State police is here."

Lieutenant Marsh motioned at Henry. "This is Warden Barnes from Wrightsville Correctional Facility."

"Wrightsville," Larry said. "Isn't that where—"

Lieutenant Marsh said, "Yes, it is. That's why I'm here. We've tracked the two escapees to this mall."

The security guard who had led them to the office said, his voice flat, "You're shitting us."

"I'm afraid not. The state police have a limited number of men already canvassing the mall. None of them are in uniform—they're all undercover. The only reason I'm reaching out to you is because time is of the essence."

The security guard who had led them to the office said to Larry, "We should call Brad."

"Who's Brad?" Lieutenant Marsh asked.

"He's the head of security."

"That's fine, but can we take a look at your security system first? I'd like to see if we can get eyes on the escapees."

Larry was nodding, backing into the room, motioning for them to follow. "Any idea where they might be?"

Lieutenant Marsh circled the counter, Henry following, and

entered the back room. Three dozen monitors were spread out on the wall. Larry lowered himself down into a computer chair and started typing at one of the keyboards.

"We believe they're in the food court."

Larry grabbed the mouse and moved it around and brought up the food court. The place was packed.

"Like finding a needle in a haystack," muttered the other security guard.

Lieutenant Marsh said, "Is this the only security system on the premises?"

Larry nodded, clicking the mouse so that different angles of the food court popped up on the main screen.

"Stop." Lieutenant Marsh leaned forward, squinting at the monitor. He grabbed his cell phone, dialed a number, and placed it to his ear. "Sir, I think we spotted them."

28

Logan stationed himself on a bench near one end of the food court. He'd finished the pretzel and now just sipped the soda, staring down at the Samsung in his hand while making furtive glances at Sean Wescott and Ashley Gilmore. From this angle, he had a clear view of them, but they wouldn't easily see him.

He'd been sitting there for nearly an hour.

The battery on the phone was almost dead. Which meant that at any moment his line to Agent Ramirez would soon be severed.

He took another sip of his soda. Just dregs now and some ice. He tossed it into the trashcan next to the bench, stared down at the nearly dead Samsung.

The phone vibrated in his hand.

INCOMING CALL, the screen said.

He placed the phone to his ear, said, "I'm almost out of battery power."

Agent Ramirez said, "Any progress?"

"None. How far away are you?"

"Not far at all. We should be—"

The phone died, cutting her off.

"Shit," Logan muttered. He held the dead phone in his hand for a moment, then tossed it into the trashcan as well.

He stood up. He would look weird sitting on the bench with no shopping bags and no cell phone to vacuously stare at. He'd stick out, so he started walking the perimeter of the food court.

Logan had barely taken ten steps when he heard the gunshots.

"Wait," Larry said. "What the hell was that?"

They stood behind him in the surveillance room, watching the monitors.

Everyone in the food court reacted. Some had jumped to their feet. Others were diving under tables.

"Chaos," Lieutenant Marsh said.

And drew his weapon from its holster, placed the barrel against the back of Larry's head, and pulled the trigger.

It was only two gunshots, but they had the desired effect.

The frenzied crowd of Black Friday shoppers taking a break to eat became a stampede. Everyone headed for the closest exit. Pushing into each other. Knocking each other down. Trampling over one another.

Logan fought through the crowd. He started to reach for the Glock in his waistband but hesitated. The last thing he needed right now was someone spotting the gun and thinking he was the shooter.

He scanned the crowd for Sean Wescott and Ashley Gilmore. They'd vanished from their table. Logan couldn't spot the cowboy hat.

Had someone been shot?

Was someone now lying on the ground, a bullet in their chest?

Logan pushed into the crowd, swimming his way through the sea of bodies, trying desperately to spot *something*.

There—on the other side of the food court, a man in a cowboy hat. Was it Sean? At this point, Logan had nothing else to go on.

He lowered his shoulder and pressed forward against the mass.

As Larry fell forward, his blood and brains spraying the desk, Lieutenant Marsh turned and fired two rounds into the other security guard's chest.

He pivoted and aimed the pistol at Henry.

Henry stared at him, his mouth agape.

Lieutenant Marsh said, "I didn't want this to happen. I told you to stay back at the motel."

Henry found his voice. "But—but—but why?"

"I needed you to get me access to the crime scenes. I may be a state police lieutenant, but I'm far from my assigned area and they would have questioned why I was there. You gave me a reason, and I needed to know where they were headed before he finally contacted me."

"Who?"

"Sean Wescott," Lieutenant Marsh said, and fired two rounds into Henry's chest.

Sean Wescott and Ashley Gilmore hurried through the food court toward the service exit. Sean still had the Colt in his hand. He'd fired two rounds at the ceiling, didn't even raise the gun up so that it would cause too much notice. Just pulled it out, held it at waist level pointed at the ceiling, and fired twice. Everything else happened just as it had been predicted.

They weren't the only ones headed toward the service exit. Others hurried that way for cover. Sean and Ashley ignored them, their focus on getting out of the mall. But then someone noticed the Colt in Sean's hand and shouted "Gun!" and Sean turned and fired at the man. His shot was wide, the bullet grazing the man's arm. Still it was enough for the man to cry out and fall to his knee, the guy's wife or girlfriend crouching behind him for cover as she screamed.

The gunshot had also spooked the others in the corridor, causing everyone else to run away from them.

Sean and Ashley hurried forward now with nobody in front or behind them.

They turned the corner and a security guard was headed in their direction, talking frantically into a walkie-talkie. He immediately raised his hands at the sight of Sean's gun.

Sean shot him in the leg.

They ran past the guard without another glance.

Daniel Marsh used the rest of his magazine to empty bullets into the surveillance system console. The computers were far too large and many to take with him, and he didn't have time to try to access the system and delete what was there. This would have to do for now.

Once the mag was exhausted, he replaced it with a fresh one and headed back out into the security office.

He opened the door partway but didn't step out into the corridor, listening for whoever may be coming in his direction.

Someone was coming his way.

Two people by the sound of it.

Daniel stepped out of the office just as the footsteps neared the corner. He aimed, his finger on the trigger, ready to fire.

Sean Wescott and his girlfriend appeared.

They stopped at once, Sean Wescott raising his own gun. But then Sean recognized Daniel and lowered the gun.

"Where are you parked?" Sean asked.

"Right outside."

They hurried down the corridor to the exit. Daniel peeked outside. The area was deserted.

He headed straight for the cruiser. He used the key to open the trunk, which contained clothes for Sean and Ashley.

Sean Wescott climbed into the trunk, followed by Ashley. It was tight, but they managed to fit.

Before Daniel closed the trunk, he said, "Where to?"

"South," Sean Wescott said. "Head south."

Logan hurried down the corridor, the Glock out now, following the trail of wounded bodies.

He came to the security office, peeked inside, saw nobody, and continued on.

The door at the end of the corridor slid open as he approached.

Logan stepped out, the Glock half-raised, scanning the parking area for Sean Wescott or Ashley Gilmore.

Nothing.

There were some vehicles parked around the area, some trucks and mall security SUVs.

He approached them slowly, quietly, his gaze skipping behind the vehicles and under the vehicles and at anywhere the two may be hiding.

Sirens rose in the distance.

The police would be here any minute.

A sound behind him.

Logan spun, the Glock raised.

Two sets of dumpsters sat against the wall.

He approached, his gaze steady on the dumpsters.

Someone was definitely hiding behind them.

Logan could hear the shallow breathing.

"Come out," he said.

Nothing.

"Come out or I'll shoot!"

"Okay, okay!" shouted a terrified voice behind the dumpsters.

There was the shuffling of feet on the pavement as a teenager stumbled out, his hands raised above his head. He wore a Burger King uniform.

"Please don't shoot me," the kid said, near tears.

"Is there anybody else back there?"

The kid frowned. "What?"

"Is there anybody else back there with you?"

"No, just me. I ran out here when I heard the shots."

"Did anybody come out here in the past five minutes?"

"I heard some people. Didn't see them, but I heard them get in a car. Someone asked someone else where they were headed. That guy said south."

"Did you see the car?"

The kid hesitated.

"*Did* you?"

"Dude, are you even a cop?"

"I'm undercover. Now answer the goddamned question."

"Yes! Yes, I saw the car. It was"—the kid swallowed—"it was a cop car."

Now it was Logan's turn to frown. Before he could say anything else, though, the sirens became almost deafening as two police cruisers tore down the ramp.

Logan dropped the gun to his side. He lowered himself to the ground, first on one knee, then on the other, tossed the gun aside, and placed his hands on the top of his head.

29

They put him in one of the holding rooms in the security office. There was nothing in the room except a bench built into the wall. This was where the security guards put shoplifters, presumably, before the local police arrived to take them into custody.

There were no windows in the room. Nothing on the walls. Just the bench built into the wall and the fluorescents in the ceiling.

Logan sat on the bench, his wrists handcuffed behind his back, his ankles shackled.

Two police officers stood guard by the door. They didn't stand guard *outside* the holding room but inside it, both with their backs to the door, their arms folded across their chests as they glared down at him.

Voices started up outside in the main lobby. Loud voices, arguing. Then the door opened and Agent Gloria Ramirez stood there in her black pantsuit. She looked around the room, first at Logan then at the two guards, and then she turned to a gray-haired man in a state police uniform.

"He's coming with us," she said.

The man shook his head vehemently. "I told you, Agent Ramirez, he isn't."

"It's Special Agent in Charge Ramirez, Major Cullen, and I'm taking custody of this man and that's final."

"The hell it is."

For the first time, both officers turned their focus away from Logan to watch the ensuing argument.

Agent Ramirez said, "After what's happened in the past forty-eight hours, what makes you think I'm going to leave this man in your custody?"

"He wasn't wanted by the feds, the last I checked."

"Maybe not, but his associate, the one who escaped with him, killed a federal agent."

Major Cullen shook his head again. "Not going to happen."

Agent Ramirez stepped forward, leaned in close. She said, her voice just above a whisper, "Are you sure you want to do this in front of your men?"

"I'm not doing anything other than ensuring you don't take our prisoner."

Agent Ramirez nodded slowly, looking around the room at the other men. She said, "Okay, listen, so this is where we're going to end up. After a lot of bickering back and forth, calling each other's superiors, this will eventually work its way up to the governor's office. The governor, as you can imagine, is not happy that two prisoners happened to escape one of his prisons, so you can believe he's willing to do anything to make sure both prisoners are apprehended as soon as possible. These men came to this mall for a reason. Why—well, we don't know that yet, but I'm sure the governor would like to know why just as everybody else. In case you haven't figured it out yet, Major Cullen, this man has information that we need."

"We'll interrogate him," Major Cullen said.

"Okay, so then let's consider another option. How many news vans are outside right now? When I came in, I saw CNN and Fox

News, and I'm pretty sure MSNBC was setting up. I don't know about you, but I'm pretty sure you don't want a federal agent—i.e., me—making a public statement about how difficult your department has been."

Major Cullen opened his mouth, but Agent Ramirez cut him off.

"Or, even worse, how your department has done nothing more than to impede this manhunt as Sean Wescott is still out there somewhere. Is that what you want the official story to be? That you decided to inflate your ego over helping capture a dangerous criminal and get him off the streets for good?"

Major Cullen didn't answer.

Agent Ramirez smiled at him, nodded. "See, I thought you might see it my way. The truth is, your department will get credit for apprehending Neal Palmer, so quite frankly I don't see what all the fuss is about."

Major Cullen said, "He killed three men here, including Warden Henry Barnes."

"Did he? Because from what I was told, the gun he was found with was fully loaded."

"He could have had another magazine or another weapon."

"True, but what about gunshot residue? Tell me, what do you think your people are going to find once they test that? Will the ballistics match his gun?"

Major Cullen said nothing.

"From what I heard—and quite honestly, I haven't heard all that much—it's pretty evident Sean Wescott did most, if not all, of the killing here. In fact, from what I understand, Neal Palmer rushed past one of the security guards who had been shot. If Neal wanted to, he could very well have ended the guard's life, but he didn't."

Major Cullen barked out a laugh. "So showing restraint is somehow commendable?"

Agent Ramirez kept her gaze steady with the major's. "In my

case," she said, "restraint should be considered very commendable, otherwise I would have punched your lights out minutes ago and saved us both the time."

She slipped a cell phone from her pocket.

"Want me to call the governor's office and get the ball rolling? I don't know about you, but I hate wasting valuable time."

Major Cullen said nothing. He glanced around the lobby, glanced back at the two police officers standing guard by the door. He cleared his throat, turning back to Agent Ramirez.

"You said the state police will get credit for the capture?"

She gave him a deadpan stare. "Do you need to clean your ears? That's what I've been saying from the start."

The major nodded, looking around at the men again. "Yes, well, I needed to be one hundred percent certain we were on the same page. This was a massacre, after all."

"No," Agent Ramirez said, her tone flat, "a massacre is what I'll do to your career if you force me to stand here one minute longer. So if I were you, I would release this man into my custody so we can work on tracking down Sean Wescott before he disappears for good."

Major Cullen said nothing at first. Then he took a breath, clapped his hands together, and turned to the two officers.

"You heard the agent," he said. "Get the son of a bitch out of here."

The two officers moved at once, advancing on Logan, grabbing his arms and pulling him to his feet. They directed him out of the room toward Agent Ramirez, who seemed to think of something else.

She raised a finger, turned back to the major. "One more thing."

30

The state police had set up a barricade for the press, keeping the news vans with their reporters and producers and cameramen far enough away from the service entrance. How they'd gotten wind this was where Neal Palmer would eventually be brought out, nobody could say, but so far several police cars had entered the service entrance and none had yet come out, so there was hope that at any minute the escapee would appear.

A helicopter circled above the mall, the local news affiliate eager for the shot that would be seen around the country.

An hour passed and nothing happened. Nobody came or went from the service entrance. Producers made frantic phone calls to local law enforcement, pleading for any small morsel of information they could feed their viewers. Reporters stood out in the frigid afternoon, bundled up in jackets, their backs to the wind as they tried to speculate what might happen next.

The only facts they had were that there'd been a shooting at the Black River Mall and that Neal Palmer—one half of the Wrightsville Duo, as some talking head had dubbed them—had been taken into custody. The magnitude of the shooting depended on which witness wanted to speak to a camera. Some stated only one person had been shot, while an outspoken few believed this was some kind of terrorist attack.

For the most part, though, it was a waiting game. The producers making their phone calls. The reporters doing everything they could to make their old news sound new during their live remotes. The helicopter circling in the air, its pilot keeping a cautious eye on the gas gauge.

Until, all at once, everybody started scrambling. The cause was unclear, but once one reporter broke away from the crowd with her cameraman trailing, the others followed suit.

A minute later, three state police cruisers came up the ramp of the service entrance. Each cruiser had two troopers occupying the front seats, but only one cruiser—the middle one—had someone in the back.

Cameramen bustled for the best view, zooming in on Neal Palmer in the backseat. He had his head down and didn't look up once as the cruisers weaved through the parking lot toward the main road, their roof lights blazing. By that point the mall parking lot had been mostly emptied, all the stores and shops closed for the day, giving the news crews more than enough room to chase after the cruiser.

The helicopter banked hard to the left, dipping low enough for the cameraman hanging out the side to get a spectacular bird's-eye view of the procession.

Everyone's focus was on the three cruisers leaving the mall parking lot and merging onto the highway, headed north to the state police barracks fifteen miles away.

It was just as Agent Gloria Ramirez had planned.

Because while everybody was in a frenzy, Logan Taylor was led out through a service corridor on the other side of the mall. He was still handcuffed, was still shackled, following Gloria and another agent he didn't know while two state troopers trailed them.

A sedan waited outside the exit, another sedan occupied by two agents parked behind it.

Logan was loaded into the backseat of the first sedan. Gloria slid into the passenger seat, the agent Logan didn't know slid behind the wheel, and a minute later they were exiting the parking lot, the other sedan following close behind.

As they neared the highway on-ramp, Gloria said, "Do you know where to?"

"South," Logan said. "Go south."

31

After five miles, when it was clear they weren't being followed, Gloria seemed to relax. Shifting in her seat to look back at him, she said, "How are you doing?"

"How the fuck do you think I'm doing?"

"You look well, all things considered."

"This whole thing has gone off the rails."

"I know."

"People have died."

"I *know*."

"What's Charles's take on all of this?"

"He's very concerned."

"I imagine I would be too if I was a Deputy Assistant Director of the FBI. Any word on Maryann?"

"None. It's difficult for us to try to get information when we can't let out that she was an active agent."

"I can't believe she would kill herself."

"Me neither. By the way"—she tilted her head at the driver—"this is Agent Thomas Paulson."

Thomas glanced at him in the rearview mirror and nodded.

Logan said, "I saw Janine driving the other car, but who's with her?"

"That would be Agent Samuel Park. Charles added him last minute."

"Did that major say Henry Barnes is dead?"

"He did, and it's true—I saw the body."

"What the hell was Barnes even doing there in the first place?"

"I'm not sure. Now, Logan, tell us what you know. All this time you've been heading north, but now we're going south. Why?"

"I think Wescott wanted to mislead the authorities. The farther north we went, the more they'd focus all their attention in that direction. Probably assumed we were heading for the Canadian border."

"Then why the shooting at the mall?"

"I'm not sure. Maybe so it adds an additional distraction. Puts the media and the authorities into an even larger frenzy."

"But how do you know south is where Wescott is now headed?"

"I don't, not one hundred percent. By the time I made it out into the service area, Sean and Ashley were gone. Speaking of which, do you have any information on her?"

"We don't. Samuel couldn't find any record of her. Though now that we have her ID"—Gloria patted the plastic bag which contained the items Logan had on him when he was taken into custody: Ashley's driver's license, several twenties, the switchblade and Glock—"maybe Samuel will have better luck."

"Sean said she was his girlfriend. Christ, Gloria, they've killed people."

"I know. That's why I have no qualms taking them out when the time comes. But explain again how you know they're headed south."

"There was a kid hiding behind the dumpster. He didn't see

Wescott, but he heard two voices, both male. One of them asked where they were going, the other said south."

"Why is this the first I'm hearing about it?"

"Maybe you should ask Major Cullen. I'm sure he withheld that information for his own purposes, though I can't imagine what they may be."

"That son of a bitch," Gloria muttered.

"There's another thing," Logan said. "The kid said he caught a glimpse of the car as it was leaving the service area."

"And?"

"He said it was a cop car."

Gloria was quiet for a moment. "You're joking."

"No."

"A fucking *cop* car?"

"That's what he said."

"I don't buy it."

"Normally I'm inclined to agree with you, but after the past twenty-four hours, there's no telling what Wescott has up his sleeve." Logan paused. "Henry Barnes had to have gotten there somehow. He wouldn't have just shown up out of nowhere."

Gloria said, "What are you thinking?"

"I think I need to give someone a call."

"Who?"

Logan told her.

Her head twisted around so quickly it was a surprise she didn't give herself whiplash.

"Absolutely not," she said.

"It has to be me."

"Why?"

"If you try to talk to him, there will be too many questions."

"And there won't be with you?"

Logan just stared at her. "Dial the number."

32

Lewis Riddell stood in the break room with several other correctional officers watching the television.

A reporter stationed in the parking lot of the Black River Mall in upstate New York told viewers that there had been a shooting at the mall, that there had been several fatalities, and that Neal Palmer had been apprehended but that Sean Wescott was still at large.

They watched aerial footage of state police cruisers taking Neal Palmer away. The footage didn't last long, going back to the reporter in the studio recapping the escape and the manhunt of the past forty-eight hours.

A phone rang.

One of the officers wandered over and grabbed the phone. Listened for several seconds, then turned and caught Lewis's eye.

"Call for you."

Lewis said, "Is it Barnes?"

"No, someone from the FBI."

Lewis stood thinking for a moment and then told the officer to transfer it to his office extension and left the break room and crossed the hallway to his office, where the phone on his desk was already ringing.

He picked it up as he circled his desk and sank down in his chair.

"This is Correctional Captain Lewis Riddell."

"Henry Barnes is dead."

Lewis shot up in his chair, his body all at once tense. "Who is this?"

"Neal Palmer. And it wasn't me. I want to make that clear from the start."

"You're supposed to be in custody."

"I need you to understand that I never wanted any of this. All the people who have died, that was never part of the plan."

"Fuck you."

"Lewis, I have a very important question to ask you."

"Fuck you."

"I wasn't the one who killed Barnes, but I want to try to figure out who did."

"Fuck. You."

"Why was he at the mall?" Neal Palmer asked. "How did he manage to track us there?"

Lewis's clenched fist loosened for an instant as he frowned. "He was at the mall?"

"I believe Sean Wescott killed him. If not Wescott, then someone who was with Wescott. Lewis, please, I need you to answer this one thing. Who was Barnes with?"

Lewis said nothing.

"Lewis?"

"Which one of you killed Maryann Webster?"

"That wasn't either of us. Like I told you, the plan was never to kill anyone."

"But you're saying Warden Barnes is dead."

"Yes."

"Murdered."

"Yes."

Lewis shot to his feet, slamming his fist down on the desk. "Fuck you!"

For a moment there was a lengthy silence.

"I don't expect you to trust me, Lewis. I don't even expect you to believe me. But I did not kill Henry Barnes. I do, however, want to find out who did."

Lewis said nothing.

"He wouldn't have just taken off," Neal Palmer said. "He would have told you where he was going. He would have told you who he was with. I need to know who."

Lewis made no reply.

"Who was the cop with him?"

Lewis blinked. "How did you know he was with a cop?"

Another silence, and then Neal Palmer said, "Tell me who it is, Lewis. Please, for the love of Christ, tell me who Warden Barnes was with. Tell me the name."

33

Agent Janine Snyder's cell phone rang.

She was driving the second sedan, trailing three car lengths behind the lead car. She pulled the phone from her pocket, saw it was Gloria, hit the button to put it on speakerphone.

"You're on speakerphone," she said.

Gloria said, "There's a safe house twenty miles away. We're going to make a quick pit stop."

Janine traded glances with Samuel.

"Everything okay?" she asked.

"Yes. I think Logan could use a break. Samuel, can you hear me?"

"Yes."

"I need you to find somebody for us as quickly as possible."

"Who?"

"Daniel Marsh. He's a lieutenant with the New York State Police We believe he's transporting Wescott. Find him ASAP."

Gloria disconnected without another word.

Samuel twisted in his seat to reach for his computer bag in the backseat. He slid out his laptop, opened the lid, powered it on.

"I'd be lying if I said I didn't feel somewhat manipulated."

Janine glanced at him. "What do you mean?"

"Two days ago I get a call from the Deputy Assistant Director that I'm needed on this operation. I find out that Sean Wescott escaped prison and that our job's to track him down and apprehend him."

"That's right."

"Then why am I only now finding out about Logan Taylor?"

Janine kept her focus on the highway. "It was classified."

Samuel snorted. "You're not joking. While we were at the mall I looked him up. According to the database, he doesn't exist."

She frowned at him. "What do you mean?"

"He's not listed as an agent anywhere."

"Of course he's not. He's undercover."

"I understand records have to be hidden for undercover agents, but what I'm saying is there *is* no record, hidden or otherwise."

Janine was quiet for a moment, taking this in. She said, "Maybe it's behind a firewall you don't have access to."

"Listen, not to sound cocky, but I'm one of the best analysts in the bureau. I can hack into any system. The reason they brought me on is because in high school I hacked into North Korea's nuclear program. I've done work at the Pentagon, and the bureau brought me on for counterterrorism. Which, to be honest, doesn't make sense why the Deputy Assistant Director requested me for this operation. This isn't terrorism."

"No, but it's high profile. Hacking into traffic cams and the like? I'm sure it's child's play for you."

"Maybe," Samuel said, now typing at the laptop. "It still feels like I'm doing bitch work."

"Hey," Janine said.

Samuel forced a smile. "Sorry, poor phrasing. But seriously, Logan Taylor—just how long was he undercover?"

"For this operation? Two years."

"How many undercover operations has he done?"

"Can't say."

"Do you know him?"

She glanced at Samuel. "What do you mean?"

"The way you talk about him, it sounds like you're friendly."

"You could say that. We went to the Academy together. Even dated briefly, but it didn't work out. Logan knew early on he wanted to do undercover work. It makes it difficult being in a relationship with someone who's gone years at a time."

"What made him sign up for this operation?"

"He had just completed another deep cover assignment when Agent Weber was killed. Once Logan found out what Wescott had done—especially how he stole the laptop—he wanted to help."

"I knew about the money, but what laptop?"

"There was a file on David Weber's laptop that consisted of every informant the FBI has."

"Jesus Christ," Samuel said. "And Wescott's had it this entire time?"

"We believe so."

"Why did David Weber have the file in the first place?"

"I'm not sure. But once Wescott was captured, he didn't have anything on him—no money, no laptop, nothing. He lawyered up right away, so we never had a chance to interrogate him, but then at the trial he pleaded guilty."

"And the money?"

"It was off the books. We had used Wescott as an informant. David had approached him about trying to buy weapons from some possible terrorists. Instead, Wescott killed David and stole the money."

"So Logan's idea was to send himself to prison?"

"That's right. The plan was to eventually break out, take Wescott along, and Wescott would lead him to the money and the laptop."

"But now everything's gone to shit."

"Yes."

"What happens when the media discovers that the bureau had a hand in helping Sean Wescott escape prison?"

Janine said nothing.

"That news comes out, there will be a thousand lawsuits. Gloria and Charles will lose their jobs. Shit, we'll *all* lose our jobs."

"That's something we'll have to worry about later," Janine said.

"Say that again?"

"We're going to catch up with Wescott, one way or another. We're going to either bring him back in or put him down. We're going to make this right."

Samuel shook his head, turning his attention back to the laptop. It was connected to the Internet and he immediately started opening the programs he needed to access the state police's database.

"All right, Lieutenant Marsh," he whispered, "where the hell are you?"

34

Traffic along the highway was backed up for almost a mile. The shoulder was open, surprisingly, and this was what Daniel Marsh took. He didn't bother with his emergency lights or his siren. He let the fact it was a state police cruiser ensure nobody tried to pull out in front of him.

After a half mile, he spotted the roadblock farther ahead. One police cruiser blocking the left lane, another cruiser blocking the shoulder. A third cruiser was parked in front of the first cruiser on the shoulder, no doubt with a trooper inside to act as the chaser in case anybody tried to make a run for it.

Four officers worked the roadblock. Two waved the cars ahead while two others peered inside at the driver and passengers and checked trunks to make sure nobody was hiding inside.

There was just enough room on the outside of the shoulder for him to squeeze past.

The four troopers working the roadblock nodded at him. Daniel nodded back. The trooper in the chase car, however, climbed out of his cruiser and walked over to him.

Daniel halted the cruiser, lowered his window.

He didn't recognize the trooper approaching him.

The trooper said, "What's the hurry?"

"What?"

"Don't you want to waste half your shift waiting in that line?"

The trooper grinned, making it clear it was a joke.

Daniel chuckled. "Yeah, I can't imagine people are happy to get stuck in that."

"They've actually been pretty good about it. They understand the reason. Say, where are you headed?"

"I volunteered to help out a buddy of mine down in Corning."

"How long you've been working?"

"Since yesterday afternoon."

"No shit? I came on last night. Been chugging Red Bulls, but they don't seem to help. Say, before you head on, can I check the trunk?"

Daniel paused, studying the trooper's face. "Seriously?"

The trooper's face remained expressionless for a long second, and then he chuckled again. "No, I'm just messing with you. Stay safe, you hear?"

"You too."

Daniel steered the cruiser back onto the highway. He kept glancing in the rearview mirror at the chase car until he had put enough distance between them that it disappeared.

He took the next exit and drove for several miles through a small town until the buildings dropped away and open fields lay out on both sides of the road, mountains in the distance.

Campgrounds were coming up. The entrance was blocked by a chain, a sign stating that the campgrounds wouldn't be open until spring.

Daniel unhooked the chain, coasted the cruiser through, got back out and hooked the chain, then got back in the cruiser.

He drove to the campgrounds. Several cottages. A few pavilions. The lake looked ready to be iced over any day now.

Daniel stepped out of the car, looked around the area to make sure nobody was around, and popped the trunk.

Sean Wescott and Ashley Gilmore lay huddled inside.

Sean peered up at him. "Where are we?"

"Campgrounds. It's okay, they're deserted."

"Are you positive?"

Daniel looked around the area once more. "Yeah, I'm positive."

"What time is it?"

"Almost seven o'clock."

"Are we still in New York?"

"Yes."

"Why?"

"I thought you could stretch your legs."

Sean didn't say anything, but the girl said, "Thank God, I need to pee."

Daniel helped her out of the trunk. He offered his hand to Sean, but he waved it away as he climbed out.

The girl headed toward one of the cottages. The door was locked, of course, but she barely paused as she disappeared behind it.

Sean Wescott said, "How much farther?"

"To the border? Another hour and a half."

"We went through a checkpoint, didn't we?"

"Yes."

"Will they have another checkpoint set up at the state line?"

"It's difficult to say."

Sean's eyes hardened, and his voice went flat. "What am I paying you for?"

"You haven't even paid me yet."

"Soon. We need to get to the money first."

"Yeah, about that. It would be a real help if you told me where we're headed."

The girl reappeared from behind the cottage, headed back their way.

Sean said, "I'm not ready to tell you yet."

The girl said, "Tell him what?"

"I need to know where we're going," Daniel said. "Otherwise I could be taking us in the wrong direction."

"You aren't. I told you to go south, and that's where you're headed."

Daniel sighed. "I understand you're not ready to trust me yet, fine, but I'm putting my neck on the line for you."

"It's more than just your neck, Daniel. Your career as you know it is over. But you're okay with that, right? As I remember our conversation, half a million dollars is enough for you to start a new life and walk away from all your gambling debts."

"It's definitely a start. No more child support. No more dealing with my ex-wife's bullshit."

Sean clapped him on the shoulder. "That's the spirit. Anything come over the radio yet?"

"Just the usual stuff so far. They apprehended your partner Neal."

"Neal Palmer is not my partner. In fact, that's not even his real name. He's FBI."

Daniel's face went white. "Jesus Christ. You could have told me this sooner."

"And when, exactly, would I have done that? Tapped Morse Code to you in the trunk?"

Daniel said nothing now, his jaw clenched.

"You got rid of your cell phone by now, I hope."

Daniel shook his head. "No, but I stripped the battery and SIM card out once we left the mall."

The girl placed a hand on Sean's arm. "You might as well tell him."

Sean studied Daniel's face for a while, finally shook his head. "No, I don't think I'm ready to trust him completely yet. But I will say this. Head toward Scranton."

"That's where the money is?"

Sean shook his head. "You disappoint me."

"I'm only trying to get a better sense of where we're headed. Otherwise, I'm driving blind."

"Fine," Sean said. "We're headed to a ghost town, Lieutenant Marsh. Does that help? We're headed to a ghost town."

35

The safe house was a ranch house sitting on the outskirts of a suburb seventeen miles from the highway. It had a two-car garage, and this was where they parked the sedans, the house agent having already moved his car to the street.

The house agent kept a hand on his holstered gun as they brought Logan inside, Logan shuffling because of the manacles around his ankles.

"Have to admit," the house agent said, "we don't get too many prisoners passing through here."

Agent Ramirez asked, "What room?"

The house agent directed them through the house to one of the bedrooms. Only there was no bed inside. There was a metal table with hooks to latch suspects, two chairs facing each other on both sides.

They sat Logan down, secured his ankle and wrist manacles to the table. Agent Ramirez said they needed to check something online and turned to leave.

The house agent said, "Want me to stay with him?"

Janine said, "I'll keep an eye on him."

"You want company?"

"I'll be fine."

Once they were gone, the door closed, Janine sat in the chair facing Logan. They said nothing, Logan watching the table, until a minute later the door opened and Samuel poked his head in and nodded once at Janine before shutting the door again.

"There," she said, "the recording devices are off. Wish I could take the manacles off, too, but you know we need to keep them on for show."

Logan said nothing, kept staring at the table.

Janine reached across the table, squeezed Logan's hand. "Talk to me."

He shifted his eyes up to meet hers. "This whole thing has gone sideways."

"I know."

"Gloria said there's still no word on Maryann. What's that about? There's no way she killed herself."

"I know."

"Something strange is going on here," Logan said.

Janine didn't say anything. She watched Logan, her mouth slightly open, as if trying to place the words in her head in some comprehensible order.

Logan frowned at her. "What's wrong?"

"On the drive here, Samuel said something to me, something that didn't make sense."

"What?"

She hesitated again. "He said you had been ... erased."

"What are you talking about?"

"When he attempted to look you up in the database, there was nothing. Not even stuff from before you went undercover."

"That's impossible."

"That's what I told him. I said they must have put it behind some kind of firewall. After all, this operation is top secret. But Samuel still should have been able to find it."

They sat in silence for a moment.

Logan said, "Get Gloria."

Janine just sat there, watching him.

"Get Gloria," he repeated, this time with more force.

"I'm thinking we should call Charles instead."

"Even better."

Janine pulled out her cell phone and dialed Charles.

Charles answered, "This is Howell."

Janine said, "It's me. I'm here with Logan. You got a moment?"

A pause as Charles moved to another location. When he spoke next, it was a harsh whisper.

"This better be goddamned important to be calling me directly. You know any contact should be coming through Agent Ramirez."

Logan said, "I hear I've been erased from the database."

Another pause. "Who told you that?"

"Agent Park did," Janine said.

"Well, it's not true. I mean, it is true, but that's only because we needed to make sure there was no connection to Logan on the off chance Wescott had someone who could access the database. Once this is all over, getting him reinstated will be no problem, just the click of a mouse."

"What's being done about Maryann?" Logan asked.

At first Charles didn't answer. There was silence. Then when he spoke again, his voice was much more somber.

"We're doing all that we can."

"She didn't kill herself."

"Trust me, Logan, I want to believe she didn't kill herself either, but the evidence isn't looking good."

"How so?"

"No forced entry, no eyewitnesses of anybody coming or going from the house. If someone did kill Maryann and tried to make it look like a suicide, they're doing a damned fine job of it. Wait—how are you calling me anyhow?"

"We stopped at a safe house," Janine said.

"Why?"

"We need time to regroup."

"So no leads on Wescott's location?"

"We think we have one," she said. "He may have escaped with the help of a New York state trooper. Agent Ramirez is following up on that right now."

"Jesus Christ," Charles breathed. "Listen, I have to head back into a meeting, but make sure Gloria keeps me updated."

Janine said that she would and closed the phone and placed it on the table. "Better?"

"Not really. Something strange is still going on here."

"You look good, by the way."

"That's what Gloria said."

"It's true."

"People died because of me," Logan whispered.

"You didn't kill anyone."

"I broke Wescott out."

"By that definition, we're all at fault."

For the first time Logan studied Janine's hands.

"What happened to your engagement ring?"

Janine looked away. "That didn't work out."

"I figured you'd be married by now. What happened?"

"It's a cliché. He cheated on me. I found out, wanted to break off the engagement. He promised me he'd never do it again, then a year later he did."

"Where is he? I'll kick his ass."

She smiled. "Once this is all over, what's your plan? Do you want to head back out into the field?"

"Part of me wants to move to some Caribbean island and live on the beach."

She smiled. "I never took you for a beach bum."

"Me neither, but there's something simplistic in it, getting away from everyday life. Not have to worry about everyday bullshit."

"Simple," Janine said. "That sounds nice."

There was a brief knock at the door.

Agent Ramirez poked her head in. "We need to go."

Janine grabbed her cell phone as she stood. "Wescott?"

Gloria nodded. "We think we know where he's headed next."

36

Daniel Marsh was tense as he approached the Pennsylvania-New York state line. Traffic was sparse, as it was expected to be as this wasn't a major throughway. By now the sun had to set, shadows stretched across the landscape.

No roadblocks were set up on the state line.

Daniel crossed into Pennsylvania with no problem. He made a U-turn a quarter mile farther down and headed back into New York.

A half mile later he turned off the highway onto a county road, the macadam having not been maintained for decades. Out here the ramshackle houses were spread apart.

One building in particular caught his eye—a body shop that looked like it had seen its last customer a decade ago. An old Coke machine sat out front displaying an outdated logo. The building's windows were dirty, though there was light inside. Hanging in the window of the entrance was an OPEN sign.

Daniel slowed to a stop. He scanned the road farther down for other houses, then glanced over his shoulder at the houses behind him. There was no one in sight.

He pulled into the gravel lot and parked the cruiser behind the body shop next to a black Ford pickup truck. Killed the engine and got out, stretching his neck as he did, listening to the joints pop.

He popped the trunk but didn't open it.

From inside, Sean Wescott whispered, "What's wrong?"

"Nothing," he said. "Gonna be right back."

Just as he got to the front of the body shop, the door opened and an old man stepped out.

"Oh, hello, Officer. Thought I'd heard a car pull in. What can I help you with?"

The man looked to be in his late-sixties, skinny as a rail, his hands stained with grease. He wore coveralls stained just as badly with the name PETER stitched across the left breast.

He pulled off a plain blue baseball cap, ran his greasy fingers through his greasy hair, reset the cap, and squinted at Daniel.

"Everything okay?"

"Hopefully," Daniel said. He surveyed the area again, making sure nobody was out and about. "You hear about the prison break?"

"Sure did. Crazy thing. That why you're here?"

"We're checking all businesses near the state line."

"You think they've made it this far already?"

"Hard to tell. Who else is working?"

"Nobody but yours truly. About to close up. You need to check the place out?"

"I do. Hope you understand."

"Of course," Peter said. He grinned. "I wouldn't feel right paying my taxes if you civil servants weren't doing your jobs."

Daniel followed the mechanic into the shop. There didn't appear to be any rhyme or reason to the set up. Invoices were scattered all over the counter.

"Please ignore the clutter," Peter said. "The maid hasn't been here today yet."

Daniel smiled at the joke as he followed Peter through the backroom and into the bay area.

The bay could hold up to three cars. Only one of them was currently occupied with a 1999 Toyota Corolla.

"Business could be better," Peter said, by way of explanation. "You need to check the trunk or something?"

Daniel shook his head. "That your pickup out back?"

"Yes, sir, it is."

"You said you're about ready to close up shop?"

"That's right."

"What time's the wife expecting you home?"

"I'm sorry?"

"Your wife," Daniel said, and gestured at the wedding band on the old man's greasy finger.

"Ah, this." The man touched the ring, began moving it back and forth on his finger. "Cathy passed away four years ago. Just never found the will to take it off, if you can understand that. You wear something so long—for us it was thirty-eight years—it becomes part of you. So I've been wearing it ever since."

"I'm sorry to hear that," Daniel said. "I guess it must be tough living alone."

Peter nodded, offering up a heavy sigh. "That it is. Every night I cook myself a TV dinner, one of those Hungry Man meals. I got a tray I set up to watch the news from the couch."

"I'm sorry," Daniel said.

"Ain't your fault."

"Yes," Daniel whispered, slipping the switchblade from his pocket, "it is."

37

It was almost nine o'clock in the evening when they passed over the New York-Pennsylvania state line on the same road Lieutenant Daniel Marsh had done so two hours previously.

Thomas and Janine had switched as drivers of the two sedans so that Gloria could update them once they were on the road. Though, honestly, there wasn't too much that needed updated. It had taken some work, but Samuel had managed to access the highway emergency cameras, tracking the moment the state police cruiser had left the mall to where it got on the highway, headed south, all the way down to the border.

Now the sedan ahead of them—Thomas at the wheel, Samuel in the passenger seat with his laptop open—pulled over to the side of the road, its taillights blazing red in the night.

Gloria grabbed the short-range walkie-talkie from the dash and hit the toggle button.

"What's wrong?"

Samuel's voice came through: "This is as far as I can track them."

"Tell me you're joking."

"I've checked as many cameras farther down this highway as I could. The cruiser never passes by."

Logan still had his ankles manacled, his wrists bound behind his back. He ducked his head to check the surrounding area.

"They were testing the border," Logan said.

Gloria glanced back at him. "Of course they were. But how does that help us?"

"Marsh knew he couldn't keep driving that cruiser much farther into Pennsylvania. He could drive it all over New York and it wouldn't raise any eyebrows, but the moment it crossed into another state, people would notice and the last thing they want right now is to be noticed."

"And?"

"I think once they determined there was no road block on the state line, they looped back to ditch the cruiser and find another form of transportation."

"Perfect," Gloria said dryly. "So now where do we start?"

Logan nodded at the walkie-talkie, and Gloria extended it back to him and hit the toggle again.

He said, "Samuel, how far back is the last camera that shows the cruiser headed in this direction?"

There was a brief pause on the other end as Samuel checked his laptop. "A half mile."

"And not once did the cruiser head past it again headed in the other direction?"

"No."

Logan said to Gloria, "So there we go. Somewhere between here and that camera they ditched the cruiser."

"But"—she shook her head, trying to work the problem out in her mind—"where?"

Logan looked around, out the windows again, at the few houses and buildings along the highway.

"It would be some kind of garage. There's no way they'd keep the cruiser out for anyone to see. Even trying to ditch it behind some trees would be risky. Too much chance of someone happening upon it. Someone finds an empty police cruiser in a place it shouldn't be, they're apt to call the police. Marsh and Wescott don't want that. So they're going to hide it."

They were quiet for a moment, mulling this over.

Janine said, "Ask Samuel if there are any businesses nearby that would have garages, like auto repair shops."

Gloria said into the walkie-talkie, "Samuel, can you check the area between us and the last camera a half mile back for any businesses with garages or something that they could use to hide the cruiser?"

"Sure, give me a minute."

Logan said, "It's not just ditching the cruiser. They'd need to replace it with something. I can't imagine Marsh already had a vehicle down here waiting for them. Then again, I didn't see someone like Marsh even factoring into this, so maybe Wescott had something else up his sleeve. For all we know, maybe they had a Pennsylvania trooper waiting for them right across the border. The trooper could take them anywhere in the state."

There was another silence, all of them thinking about this, when Samuel came back over the line.

"I found two possibilities. One's here in Pennsylvania, a body shop. That's about a quarter mile away. Another is a place back across the border, a quarter mile off the main road. That's another body shop."

"That's it?" Gloria asked.

"That's all I can find right now."

"You guys check the body shop up ahead. We'll circle back and check the other one. What's the address?"

Samuel gave her the address, and she punched it into her phone's map application and brought up the route. It was easy enough. Gloria showed the screen to Janine who put the car back in gear and did a U-turn and headed back into New York as Thomas and Samuel kept going straight.

They arrived at the body shop less than five minutes later. The place was dark.

Janine pulled into the gravel lot and circled the building. No vehicles parked in the back. Just some trash cans and a bucket filled with sand and a hundred cigarette butts, but that was it.

She pulled up in front of the body shop, right in front of the three bay doors. She put the sedan in park, and both she and Gloria stepped out of the car at the same time.

Janine pulled a flashlight from her pocket and shined the beam toward the bay doors. The windows were dirty and grimed.

She approached from an angle and leaned up on her tiptoes to peer inside the garage.

"It's here," she said.

Gloria surveyed the area, then leaned back into the sedan. "We'll be right back," she told Logan before closing the door.

The entrance door to the body shop was locked. Janine used the butt of her gun to smash the closest pane of glass and reach inside to unlock the deadbolt. They entered, their weapons now drawn, both with their wrists crossed so one hand held the Glock, the other a flashlight.

Gloria checked the back room as Janine continued toward the garage. There was little concern that someone was waiting in the dark. By now Wescott would want to be long gone, not lurking in the shadows on the off chance someone happened to stumble across the stashed cruiser.

Janine slipped through the door, sliding the flashlight beam all over the garage. Besides the cruiser and a Toyota Corolla, a man lay dead in a pool of blood. He lay on his back, which made it easy for Janine to see the stab wounds in his stomach and throat.

She did a quick circuit of the garage to make sure there were no other bodies and then crouched over the dead man as Gloria entered the garage.

"Son of a bitch," Gloria murmured.

Janine pulled out the old man's wallet, began flipping through it. She slid out his driver's license.

"Call Samuel and see what information he can find about this man. There's a good chance they took his vehicle."

Gloria looked around the garage. "Assuming they didn't take a vehicle that was already here for service."

"That should be easy to check. Then again, based on all the invoices littering the counter out there, maybe not. But whatever they have planned, it's going to happen quick."

"What makes you say that?"

"Assuming the garage has weekend hours, they know this body will be found in the morning. Even if the garage doesn't open until Monday, his family will come looking for him if he doesn't show up this evening. Wescott and Marsh plan to be far away from here by the time that happens."

Gloria nodded slowly, staring down at the body. "There isn't any need, though."

Janine frowned at her. "What do you mean?"

"Remember how Logan said Wescott has things hidden up his sleeve? Well, so do I." She held up her cell phone, a fresh text message on the screen. "I know exactly where they're headed."

38

"Centralia," Daniel Marsh said, rolling the word around on his tongue. He shook his head. "Never heard of the place."

Sean Wescott lit a cigarette. "No reason you should."

They were in Pennsylvania now. It was ten thirty, the night black, and they sat parked in the old man's pickup truck alongside another county road. Ashley had needed to use the bathroom, but there were no places for them to stop, certainly not at a gas station or convenience store, so they opted for the middle of nowhere again. And while she had been gone, Sean finally decided to confide in Daniel the location of where they were headed.

"You said we were headed to a ghost town," Daniel said.

Sean nodded. "That's right."

"Centralia is a ghost town?"

"In a manner of speaking."

"What does that mean?"

"You'll see when we arrive."

"How far away is it?"

Sean took a moment to run the calculation through his head.

"About another two hours. Three hours tops, if we continue with the back roads."

"How do we get there?"

"We keep doing down 15 toward Williamsport, then cross over the Susquehanna River in Northumberland."

"How is it a ghost town?"

"You seriously never heard of Centralia?"

Daniel shook his head.

"A mine fire's been burning underneath the town since 1962."

"That was fifty years ago."

"Yes, and the fire's been going ever since. Everyone in town was forced to leave. Well, there were a few people staying behind the last I knew, maybe a dozen, maybe less."

"Everyone was forced to leave?"

"Eminent domain," Sean said. "It's a bitch of a thing."

"And that's where you hid the money?"

"Well, not quite."

"What the hell does that mean?"

"It means Centralia is where we're headed next."

"I feel like you keep yanking my chain."

"I understand that, Lieutenant Marsh, but keep in mind I have trust issues."

"What makes you think I don't have trust issues too? If this doesn't work out, I'm going to spend the rest of my life in prison."

"It'll work out."

"How can you be so positive about all this?"

"When you're running from the law, you have no choice but to stay positive. Pessimism will kill you."

A tap came from the passenger-side door.

Sean Wescott stepped out of the pickup so that Ashley could crawl across the bucket seat to squeeze in the middle. He flicked the cigarette into the grass, stepped back in, shut the door, and drummed his fingers on the dashboard.

"All right, let's go."

39

It took them two and a half hours before they arrived at Centralia. By then it was nearly one o'clock in the morning.

"Doesn't look like much, does it?" Sean said as they slowly moved through the streets. "Especially in the dark, you can't tell where the houses used to stand. In daytime it's easier to spot some of the foundations. There are even some telephone poles still standing here and there. When it gets really cold, you can see steam coming out of pockets around the area."

Graffiti marked the road in several places. As they passed a gated cemetery, the pickup's headlights splashed large shaky letters in white on the macadam.

WELCOME TO THE UNDERWORLD

"Some of the caskets have been relocated," Sean said, "most of the others haven't. The ground is beginning to buckle in spots. Years ago I walked through there and some of the grave markers were beginning to fall over. Little by little the earth's shifting and falling in on itself. That's why they kicked everyone out."

"Looks like we passed one house already," Daniel said.

"Yes, and there are a handful of others still in town."

"Why?"

Sean shrugged. "For some people, this is their home. I don't think you can explain it much more than that."

"Now where are we headed?"

"Turn left up at the next road."

Daniel checked his rearview mirror on instinct. Nobody behind them. Nobody had been behind them for miles.

"How'd you find out about this place, anyway?"

"I honestly can't remember. I think maybe I read about it in the newspaper, or maybe I saw an article about it online. Places like this have always fascinated me."

"Ghost towns?"

"Not just ghost towns. Any place in the country—in the world—where the earth has begun to takeover. Where did you grow up, Lieutenant Marsh?"

"Elmira, New York."

"Has it changed much since you were a boy?"

"Sure."

"But I bet it's changed for the better, right? They've built new businesses, new houses. People keep trying to make things better. If you wanted to—if you weren't a wanted man—you could return there any time you wanted and see the house you grew up in and the school you attended and places you hung out with your friends. But then you have a place like this town that doesn't even exist anymore. People who grew up here can't return with their own kids to show them where they grew up and what schools they attended. I mean, sure, they *can* bring their kids here, but what is there for the kids to see? I'm by no stretch an environmentalist, but you can never predict what the earth is going to do. One day it may just decide it wants its land back and will take it. There's nothing you or me or anybody can do about it."

Daniel had made the left and was now coasting down the street, open fields on either side of them.

"Now where are we headed?"

Sean pointed out the windshield. "See the church up there on the hill?"

"Yes."

"It's time we found Jesus."

Daniel placed the pickup in park, killed the engine. He'd turned off the headlights when they started up the hill to the church so that they wouldn't draw attention. Not that there was anybody around that might notice. Besides the few houses spread out around the ghost town, the area was deserted. Now the three of them sat in the pickup staring out at the white church perched on top of the hill overlooking the town that the earth had reclaimed.

"In there?" Daniel asked.

"Yes," Sean said.

"You hid one and a half million dollars in that church?"

"No."

Daniel looked at him. "I'm getting tired of your bullshit."

Sean stared out through the windshield. "One and a half million dollars is a lot of money. If I buried it somewhere, what stops someone else from stumbling over it and taking it as their own?"

Daniel said, "I'm beginning to lose my patience."

"Keep calm, Lieutenant Marsh. By this time tomorrow, you will be a half million dollars richer and sipping margaritas on a beach somewhere." Sean patted Ashley's thigh, squeezed it tight. "Now let's go get closer to God."

There were two entrances to the church, a front door that overlooked the remains of the town and a back door.

They used the back door.

Sean forced it open and led them inside. They each carried a flashlight. Once the door was closed, they flicked on the flashlights and swung the beams around the anteroom.

Coatracks stood bare in each corner of the room. Empty hangers hung from the pole along the wall. A small table with brochures and other literature about the church.

They moved deeper into the church, through the anteroom and into the chapel.

Based on the number of pews, the church didn't look like it could hold more than two hundred people.

Daniel asked, "What are we here for?"

Sean aimed his flashlight at the cross hanging against the wall at the front of the church.

"Like I told you, Lieutenant Marsh, it's difficult to make one and a half million dollars in cash disappear. Or if you do, it's difficult to make sure it's secure. That's why Ashley and I worked out a system. She put the money someplace secure and gave me the key, and I took that key and hid it. I've known where the money's been all this time, just as Ashley has, but she can't access the money without the key, and only I've known the location of that key."

They moved down the aisle to the front of the church. At both ends were narrow steps that led down to the basement. Sean climbed to the lectern.

"This church," he said, "has been one of the mainstays of the town since everything had gone to hell. Even if those other residents eventually moved out and there was nobody living in town, this church would still be here. Last I knew it still held regular services every Sunday. People drive in from outside towns to worship here. Which is kind of ironic, if you think about it, people leaving their prosperous towns to a church overlooking a town that God has decided should no longer exist."

He turned back to the cross on the wall. It stood eight feet tall from top to bottom, made from a solid piece of rugged wood. It was clamped against the wall, but the clamps weren't that secure. All it took from Sean was several yanks before the clamps loosened and gravity pulled the cross forward off the wall. It crashed down with a vicious impact that caused the lectern to tip over into the aisle.

"Jesus Christ," Daniel said.

"Quiet," Sean said. "He might hear you." Then he grinned. "If I had a religious bone in my body, I might feel bad about doing that, but as it is, I haven't been to church since I was a kid."

He picked up his flashlight and shined the beam at the top of the cross. Taped there was the key.

"When I put it here two years ago," Sean said, "I used a ladder. I also made sure when I broke in not to leave a trace. But I figure now"—he shrugged—"what the hell?"

He bent and tore the key from the top of the cross, and as he stood back up, the chapel lights came on to reveal Agent Gloria Ramirez standing at the top of the aisle, her weapon aimed directly at Sean.

40

Daniel and Ashley spun, both drawing their guns and aiming them at Gloria.

Sean Wescott didn't react so quickly—he gazed at the key pinched between his fingers, then tossed the flashlight aside and grabbed the Colt. Didn't aim it at Gloria, but held it at his side almost casually.

"Hello, Agent Ramirez."

She said, "You don't look surprised."

"At this point, not much surprises me anymore. Actually, I take that back. I'm surprised he's not here too."

"I'm here," Logan said, stepping up from the stairwell on the wing of the church. Like Gloria, he had his Glock aimed at Sean.

At the same moment, Thomas stepped up from the stairwell on the other wing of the church, also aiming his Glock at Sean.

Daniel and Ashley took a step back, pivoted their bodies so that they could watch both Gloria at the top of the aisle and either Logan or Thomas at the wings. Daniel put a bead on Thomas, Ashley a bead on Logan.

Sean aimed the Colt at Gloria. "Looks like we've got ourselves a good ole Mexican standoff."

"Where is it?" Gloria said.

"Where's what? The money?" Sean tilted his head, his gaze steady with Gloria's. "Or the flash drive?"

Gloria said nothing.

Sean grinned, his eyes shifting to Logan. "She never told you about the flash drive, did she?"

"Put down the weapons," Gloria said.

"She gave you some bullshit story about taking Agent Weber's laptop, whatever that's about."

Gloria said, "Where is it?"

Sean looked at her again. He stared a moment, then glanced at both Logan and Thomas.

"Do either of you know what kind of person Agent Ramirez is? I'm not talking what kind of agent she is—she didn't make Special Agent in Charge for doing nothing—but I mean, really, beneath the surface where her heart and soul lie, that kind of person."

"Sean Wescott," Gloria said, "you're under arrest."

This caused Sean to bark out a laugh. "Good one, Gloria. If you keep up with the jokes, I might piss myself laughing. But seriously, Logan, part of me always assumed you were working for Gloria. I didn't want to believe it, but better safe than sorry, right? And, well, when you brought up Weber's laptop"—Sean shook his head—"I'll admit that threw me for a second."

Gloria said, "Put down your weapons or we will be forced to open fire."

"You'd like that, wouldn't you? The only problem is you can't. Because I still have the flash drive. That's been my lifeline these past two years, making sure you didn't have me taken out while I was in prison. You don't want the world to know who you are, Gloria, do you?"

She didn't answer.

Logan said, "It's over, Sean. Put the weapons down. We can end this peacefully."

Sean barked out another laugh. "Jesus Christ, you're naïve. If you haven't realized it yet, Logan, you've been used."

There was a lengthy silence, Sean surveying the chapel again, his gaze settling on Gloria.

"Story time, Agent Ramirez. You mind if I share?"

She said nothing.

"Of course you don't mind. Why would you? I'm the criminal here, the murderer, while you're Special Agent in Charge Gloria Ramirez. I break the law while you uphold it. Which makes this story even more ironic, once you get down to the nitty-gritty. Here are the basics, because I'm guessing we don't have much time. As is commonly known, I was an informant for the FBI. Because of my connections with some unsavory Russian individuals, Agent Weber approached me about making a weapons purchase. Not just a few weapons, but a lot of weapons. He said he would give me one and a half million dollars for the swap. This, as you know, was money taken out of the bureau's vault or wherever you guys keep your cache of money for bullshit deals like this. So I meet with Agent Weber to pick up the money. And that, my friends, is where this story takes an interesting turn.

"You see, there never was any deal. The whole thing was bullshit. Agent Weber told me as much right before he tried to kill me. He was bragging about it. The idea had been to set up a weapons swap, make me the go between guy, then kill me and make me disappear and play it off as if I had managed to abscond with one and a half million dollars. Meanwhile, they'd chop up my body or soak it in acid, or do whatever the cool kids are doing nowadays, and take that money for their very own. What they hadn't planned on, though, was that I'd staked out the meeting place beforehand and set up a camera. I just had a weird feeling there was something off, and I wanted to get it on camera in case

I ever needed to cover my ass. Which thankfully I did, because then Weber tried to shoot me. But I was too fast for him. I managed to knock the gun out of his hand, grabbed my gun and shot him in the stomach. Gloria, any objections to the story so far?"

She didn't answer.

"So as you can imagine, I got the hell out of there. Grabbed the money first, yeah, but the camera I left behind. Thing was, I had the recording going straight to a cloud-based server where I could access it any time anywhere. Good thing I did, because that's how I saw Agent Ramirez later arrive at the scene. Just in time too, because Agent Weber was still alive. All she needed to do was call an ambulance. And she did call somebody—I watched her get out her cell phone, put it to her ear, talk briefly—but it wasn't for an ambulance. An ambulance didn't show up for, what, two hours? By that point poor Agent Weber bled out. So yes, in a way I did kill him, but it was simply in self-defense. Could I have provided that testimony during court? Of course, but what would have been the point?"

"If what you're saying is true," Logan said, "and for the record I don't believe any of it, why not use the video as your defense?"

Sean grinned again. "Like I said, Logan, you are naïve. I could have easily uploaded the video to YouTube, sent a score of digital copies to the media. But by keeping it on a flash drive—by alerting Gloria to the fact that I had such a video—I knew I was safe for as long as that flash drive was hidden. Tell me, how did you manage to track us here anyhow? I'd like to think we did a pretty good job covering our tracks."

Gloria said, "We had help."

"From who?"

"Me," Ashley said, swinging the barrel of her Glock away from Logan and aiming it at Sean.

41

Her Glock now trained on Sean Wescott, Ashley Gilmore walked backward up the aisle toward Gloria.

"You bitch," he said.

Ashley shrugged. "Sorry, babe, but I can't be on the run for the rest of my life."

"You're giving up a lot of money."

"No, I'm not. There's a reward for you. It's more than enough, and they'll give me immunity."

Daniel Marsh didn't seem to know who to level his weapon on. He kept his pistol aimed at Thomas but he was watching Ashley now, his eyes wide, his jaw working.

Sean said, "Who gave you this deal? *Agent Ramirez?*" He shook his head. "You're making a mistake."

Gloria said, "She contacted me the day you escaped. Said she was supposed to meet up with you and offered you up for immunity and a reward. Truth was, I didn't believe it because as far as I knew, you didn't have a girlfriend, but my interest was piqued and I told her to keep in contact. She didn't until a few hours ago when she texted me this location. We'd been waiting here in the dark for over an hour before you showed up."

Sean shook his head again in disgust. "You fucking bitch."

Ashley didn't say anything. She kept moving backward up the aisle until she had almost reached Gloria.

"That's far enough," Gloria said.

Ashley whipped her face back, frowning. "But—"

"Put the gun down."

Ashley gave Sean one last look before she bent and placed the Glock on the carpet and stood back up and slowly made her way back toward Gloria.

"Stop right there," Gloria said. Keeping her own weapon leveled on Sean, she used her free hand to give Ashley a quick pat down to ensure she wasn't carrying any further weapons. "Now go outside with your hands up."

"But you said—"

"You'll still get your deal. There are two agents outside. They'll keep you safe until we get this all sorted out."

Sean Wescott shouted, "You're making a mistake."

As Ashley moved past her, Gloria said, "No, she's not."

Sean smiled. There was something cold in his smile, something calculating. His gaze steady with Gloria's, he said, "I wasn't talking to her."

By that point Ashley had grabbed the switchblade she had hidden in her boot, released the blade, and plunged it straight into Gloria's back.

The sudden strike was enough for Gloria's body to tense and her finger to tighten around the trigger. Her pistol discharged a round that hit Sean Wescott in the chest.

At the same instant, Daniel fired at Thomas who fired a half second later at Daniel. Daniel's bullet took off the side of Thomas's face while Thomas's bullet went straight into Daniel's neck.

Despite the knife still in her back, Gloria wasn't down yet.

She'd fallen to one knee but managed to keep her balance, enough so that she fired off two more rounds up at the podium.

Sean Wescott had dropped to a knee due to the first shot. He struggled to return several more rounds at Gloria. None of his bullets hit Gloria, though. One of them did hit Ashley in the shoulder. She fell back, then quickly scrambled to her feet, grabbed the knife still in Gloria's back, yanked it out and went to strike again.

Logan was already advancing up the aisle, his weapon aimed. The moment Ashley went to plunge the knife a second time, he fired two rounds into her chest. But it was too late. The knife drove deep into the top of Gloria's spinal column.

Janine and Samuel hurried into the chapel, their weapons raised, to find Logan standing in the middle of the aisle, moving in a circle.

The two agents stopped short to take in the carnage.

"What happened?" Janine said.

Logan shook his head. It was clear both Gloria and Ashley were dead, as were Thomas and Daniel. The only one still alive was Sean Wescott, up on the podium, lying half on the cross, wheezing. The Colt had fallen from his hand when he fell and lay several feet away.

When Logan stepped up onto the podium, Sean smiled at him, blood in his mouth. He kept wheezing. His right hand, the one holding the key, lifted slowly, shaking, as if a peace offering to Logan.

Logan took the key.

Sean only nodded. His wheezing grew shallower. He lay there half on the cross, blood oozing from his chest, and stared up at Logan until his eyes lost focus and he stopped breathing completely.

42

"Now what?" Samuel said. "Now just what the hell do we do?"

For a long moment nobody answered him. They stood in the chapel, looking around at the dead bodies.

Finally Logan said, "We need to call the police."

"No," Janine said. "We should call Charles first."

"What's *Charles* going to do?" Samuel said. He sounded near hysterical. "This whole thing is fucked up. Jesus Christ, Paulson and Ramirez are *dead*."

Janine already had her cell phone out, dialing Charles.

"Is the money even here?" Samuel asked.

Logan held up the key. "No money. Just this."

Samuel squinted from where he stood across the chapel. "What is that?"

Before Logan could reply, Janine said, "Yes, sir, this is Agent Snyder. We have a situation." She listened a moment, nodding, and said, "I'm going to put you on speakerphone."

She hit the button and held the phone out in front of her, Logan stepping off the podium to meet her.

"What is it?" Charles said.

"Sir," Logan said, "Gloria and Thomas are dead. So are Sean Wescott and Ashley Gilmore and Lieutenant Marsh."

There was a brief silence, then Charles said, "What happened?"

"Gloria seemed to believe Ashley Gilmore had flipped on Wescott. That's how we arrived here to the church in Centralia, by a text sent to Gloria from Ashley. But it was a double cross. Ashley ended up stabbing Gloria in the back. That's when everyone else opened fire."

Another brief silence.

"What was at the church?"

"A key."

"Do we know to what?"

"At this moment, no."

Janine said, "It looks to be a safe deposit box key."

"Do we know the location of said safe deposit box?"

"We do not," Logan said, but then paused, thinking about it. "Actually, I may have an idea, but right now that's not important. What's protocol in this situation?"

"There is no protocol," Charles said. "This operation was not strictly on the books. If all went well, the bureau would be able to take credit, but now ... Christ, I can't believe this has happened."

Logan traded glances with Janine and Samuel. He said to phone, "So what should we do, sir?"

Silence.

"Sir?"

Charles cleared his throat. "We have a problem."

"Did you say problem, sir?"

"After Janine called me earlier today, I did some snooping. It made no sense why you would be deleted from the database. So I looked into that but couldn't find anything. Then I checked everyone else working this operation. Except for Agent Ramirez, you've all been deleted."

Samuel said, his voice tense, "That's not possible."

"Don't you think I know that? At least, it *shouldn't* be possible, but somehow it is. It makes no sense why Agent Ramirez would still be listed if the rest of you aren't."

"Actually," Logan said, "it might."

"Explain."

"Before everything fell apart, Wescott claimed he had been set up by Agent Weber. That the plan was to kill Wescott and dispose of his body and steal the money."

"That's ridiculous," Charles said.

Logan said, "I know, sir, but Wescott claimed to have the whole thing recorded on video. He said that he had shot Agent Weber but that Weber wasn't dead by the time he took off. He said—" Logan paused, taking a breath. "He said that Gloria arrived not too long after, that she took in the scene and did nothing to save Agent Weber."

"That's a serious allegation, Agent Taylor," Charles said.

"I'm aware of that, sir. But Wescott also claimed he never took Agent Weber's laptop."

"Clearly the man was lying."

"Maybe so. But what if he wasn't?"

There was another brief silence.

Charles said, "It doesn't matter. This operation is over. Alert the local authorities to what's happened. I'll send over field agents ASAP. We'll get everything straightened out."

He disconnected without saying another word.

For a moment nobody spoke.

Then Samuel said, "Do you really know the location of the safe deposit box?"

Logan glanced down at the key in his hand. "I might."

Janine said to Samuel, "What are you thinking?"

"I just ... this whole thing is fucked up, but we're *so* close."

"What do you mean?" Logan asked.

"The point of this operation was to have Wescott lead us to the money and laptop, right?"

"The operation is over."

"No shit," Samuel said. "But what if it's true? What if there *is* a flash drive?"

Logan glanced down at the key again. "It doesn't matter. Once this is all sorted out, they'll trace the key to the right box. If there is a flash drive, it'll be found."

"Fuck," Samuel said. "You don't see it, do you?"

Logan traded glances with Janine.

Janine said, "See what?"

"Assuming Wescott was telling the truth, Gloria couldn't have been the only one involved in this. Why the fuck would she delete all of us from the system except herself? *How* would she manage to do that on her own?" Samuel shook his head. "No, her plan was for all of us to die. We'd find the money and the laptop—assuming there even *is* a laptop—and then Gloria or whoever she was working with would kill us."

Logan said, "You're being paranoid."

"Am I? Fine, then let's just wait here until the cops show up. As far as they're concerned, you're Neal Palmer. Janine and I can try to explain to them that you're really an undercover agent, but as of this moment, *we're* not even technically agents. Do you see yet just how fucked this is?"

Logan glanced at Janine. "What do you think?"

Janine said, "I think I want to believe Gloria wasn't capable of letting David Weber die."

"But what if she was?"

"Then I think that's something we need to know for sure. And if there is somebody else out there who was working with Gloria"—Janine shook her head, looking around at the dead bodies splayed about the chapel—"then I think we need to get to that flash drive before they do."

43

They'd parked the sedans in a clearing farther up the hill, back far enough from the road that there shouldn't have been any reason for traffic passing by to spot the cars. Not that there was much fear of that in this town—besides the few houses still standing which were dark at this time of night, the place was deserted. Still, there was a chance somebody may have heard the shooting and had already called 911.

Logan opened the passenger door of the one sedan, the one Gloria had been riding in today, and checked the glove compartment. There was the plastic baggy that the police in New York had given her from the mall: one hundred twenty dollars in cash, Ashley Gilmore's debit card and ID, and the switchblade.

Logan handed Samuel the debit card and ID. "Can you access her bank account?"

"Of course."

Samuel hurried over to the other sedan and pulled out his laptop, flipped open the lid and powered it on and waited for it to connect to the Internet.

"Holy shit," Samuel said.

Janine asked, "What's wrong?"

"Charles was right. We have been deleted. Part of me didn't want to believe it."

Samuel had set Ashley Gilmore's ID and debit card on the hood of the sedan so he could give the laptop his full attention. Logan pointed at them now.

"What about those?"

Samuel didn't react at first, staring at the laptop screen. He blinked, looked up at Logan, then down at the ID and debit card.

"Yeah, give me a minute."

Logan realized he was still gripping the switchblade and shoved it in his pocket. From his other pocket he produced the key Sean Wescott had offered him right before he died.

"So if Ashley knew where the money was this entire time," he said, "why didn't she just take it while Wescott was in jail?"

Janine said, "Maybe he had threatened her, told her that he'd hunt her down if she betrayed him. Or there's a very good chance Ashley couldn't access the money, not without the key. She'd have to tell the bank she lost it, and that's a whole process. They send in somebody to drill access to the safe deposit box. There's a good chance the money wouldn't be seen by anybody at the bank, but that would have been a lot of eyes on Ashley. And then what would she have done, decided she didn't want the box? Banks don't take chances anymore. They'd certainly remember if Ashley needed them to drill to access the box and then closed out her account. More likely she would get a new box, and then maybe access it every month, take out a few hundred thousand dollars here and there. Or maybe there's a simpler reason."

"What's that?"

"Maybe she was truly in love with him."

For a moment there was a silence, Logan and Janine staring at one another, and then Samuel spoke.

"I'm in. She opened the account two years ago, right before

Wescott was captured. There wasn't much activity—just a few transactions every month to make sure the account didn't go dormant—and every year one hundred fifty dollars was taken out as a fee. It even says here it was for SDB, which I'm assuming means safe deposit box."

"Where's the location?" Logan asked.

"Lanton, Pennsylvania. About two hours south of here."

"Do they have Saturday hours?"

Samuel tapped around on the website and nodded. "They open at eight and close the doors at three."

"Then we better hurry if we want to make it there by opening."

"Wait," Janine said. "How are we supposed to access the box? Ashley Gilmore is dead."

"That's right, she is." Logan picked up the ID, tilted it to get a good view of Ashley's picture in the moonlight. Short dark hair, glasses. He looked at Janine. "But you're not."

44

They stopped at a 24-hour Walmart in St. Clair. Logan parked the sedan not too close to the building but not too far away either, what seemed a comfortable distance among the smattering of other vehicles in the lot.

Logan waited in the sedan while Janine and Samuel hurried inside to get supplies. Fifteen minutes later they returned with two plastic bags and a black suitcase, and once they were in the sedan, Logan put it in drive and got them rolling.

They didn't speak while they drove south to Lanton. They took the back roads, all the way through Pottsville and Schuylkill Haven and Strausstown and Myerstown before they ended up in Lebanon and then Manheim. By that point it was four o'clock in the morning and they still had four hours to kill before the bank opened.

It was also around then that Charles called.

Janine put him on speakerphone so they could all hear him ask, "Where are you?"

Nobody answered.

"I have field agents at the church right now," Charles said.

"They say it's a massacre. They say the local authorities haven't even arrived yet. They say the three of you are nowhere in sight. So where the fuck are you?"

Logan said, "We decided to finish the operation."

There was a brief silence.

"No," Charles said, his voice rising in anger, "you decided to disobey a direct order."

"In a couple hours this will be over. We'll have retrieved the money and possibly the flash drive."

"There is no goddamned flash drive, Agent Taylor. Haven't you figured that out yet? Sean Wescott was lying to you."

When nobody spoke, Charles sighed.

"Had you listened to me and stayed at the church, I could have protected you. But now ... now I don't know what's going to happen."

Logan said, "We understand, sir."

"Where are you headed?"

"Lanton, Pennsylvania. Ashley Gilmore has a safe deposit box at a bank there. She opened it right before Sean Wescott was captured."

Charles sighed again. "Keep me updated on your progress," he said, and disconnected.

On the outskirts of town they found a rundown motel, much like the Green Valley Inn, in which the clerk behind the counter barely even acknowledged Janine when she paid cash for a room. The room itself was nicer than expected, two twin-size beds and a desk.

Logan used the scissors purchased at Walmart to cut two inches off Janine's hair and applied the Revlon hair color to transform her into a brunette. They waited for it to set, and once it did, Janine washed it out and put in a conditioner and dried her hair, and that was it.

They'd purchased new clothes at Walmart, too, a pair of jeans and boots and jacket and knit hat that would cover much of her head. Janine changed into them and stepped out of the bathroom, looking anxiously at the two of them.

"So how do I look?"

Logan held up Ashley's ID, comparing the photo with Janine's new look. It wasn't exact, was nowhere close to perfect, but it would do.

"Looks good," Logan said. "Samuel, how much more time do we have left?"

Samuel glanced at his watch. "Two hours."

"Then let's go over the plan one more time."

45

At seven thirty on the dot, a black Honda Civic pulled into the parking lot of Lower Penn Bank and stopped right in front of the main entrance. It waited there until a minute later another car pulled in, this one a red Saturn, and parked in one of the front spaces so that its hood faced the building. The Civic then pulled ahead and parked in one of the spaces on the side of the lot.

A man in his fifties emerged from the Civic, balding hair with a mustache and glasses. He wore a heavy jacket against the freezing morning temperature. He carried a cup of Starbucks coffee to the front entrance of the bank. Dug in his pocket for the key, unlocked the door, stepped inside, locked the door again, and then disappeared for a minute as he walked through the building. Soon he appeared again at the door, gave a quick wave, and the Saturn drifted forward to park beside the Civic.

A woman appeared from the Saturn, this one in her early thirties. She too was bundled up in a jacket and hurried across the parking lot to the entrance, where the bank manager was waiting, holding the door open for her.

"Must be the morning ritual," Samuel said. "One employee waits outside while the other checks the place out. They don't get a wave that everything's okay, the one outside calls the police."

They were parked across the street, slightly perpendicular to the bank, in a McDonald's parking lot. Samuel had gone inside and used Ashley Gilmore's cash to buy them all breakfast sandwiches. They hadn't eaten in over twenty-four hours and none of them seemed to care about the heavy odor of grease that permeated the sedan when Samuel returned with their food.

They'd been sitting there all this time, watching the bank and waiting. They watched as the bank manager and another employee—teller, costumer service rep?—moved about the bank, setting up for when they opened. Twenty minutes later another employee pulled into the lot, this one looking like a high school kid, way too chipper for this early in the morning. Five minutes later, another car pulled in, another employee, this one a woman in her twenties. College student, perhaps.

"That's four," Samuel said. He sat in the driver's seat, Logan in the passenger seat, Janine with her new look in the back. "Are you sure we should stay in the car when she goes in?"

Logan nodded, keeping his focus on the bank, an uneaten hash brown in his hand. "If she goes in by herself, where does that leave us? We could wait inside McDonald's, I guess, but if something goes down it might take too long to cross the highway to reach her."

"But won't it be suspicious, dropping her off while we sit outside in the car?"

Logan tilted his head back and forth, considering it. "We'll park on the side, right by where the employees park. With that angle we won't be noticed. Besides, she should be in and out. If everything goes according to plan, it shouldn't be more than fifteen minutes, assuming she can get in the safe deposit box with no trouble."

"Shit," Janine said. Both men turned to look at her. "I can't believe none of us thought of it."

Logan said, "Thought of what?"

"What's the box number?"

His laptop powered up again, Samuel accessed Ashley Gilmore's account, but there was nothing mentioned anywhere in her account about which number was her safe deposit box. Samuel then had to access Lower Penn's database, which took him much longer, a bank's security top of the line, designed to ensure people like Samuel couldn't access customer's information, let alone those records at the corporate office. It took him ten minutes before he issued a heavy sigh.

"Got it," he said. "Box forty-seven."

Janine, leaning forward in the backseat, her body tense, repeated the number quietly.

Logan glanced at the time on the dash. "It's eight-ten. Now or never."

There was a barrier in the middle of the highway, making it impossible for them to cross directly over to the bank. They had to make a U-turn at the next traffic light. Samuel eased into the parking lot, which now had two cars parked out front. As they pulled in, another car pulled in after them, but did not follow them to the front lot and instead drove around back to where the drive-thru was located.

Samuel slowly drove past the main entrance and kept going to the side. He stopped right at the end of the walkway.

Janine jumped out and circled back to the trunk, which Samuel popped from the latch under his seat. Janine pulled out the suitcase and slammed the trunk, and Samuel pulled ahead and parked beside the bank manager's Honda Civic, the hood pointed away from the bank so that they could watch the bank from the rearview and side mirrors.

They watched Janine as she disappeared around the corner, the suitcase in hand.

Logan once again checked the time—8:15. They'd give her fifteen minutes, and if she didn't exit the bank by then, they would know something was wrong. All they could do now was wait.

46

Just inside the glass entrance doors, Janine paused a moment to survey the bank.

Directly ahead of her was the teller line. There appeared to be space for six tellers, but this early Saturday morning there was only one. Or no—there were two, as the second teller was working the drive-thru, which could be seen through a glass partition.

Off to her right was an area with four desks. A woman sat at one, typing at a computer, while the bank manager stood near his desk, his arms crossed, listening to an old man lecture him about some sports team.

Between the teller line and the area with the four desks stood the vault. It was open now, though a glass door barred anyone access to the wall of safe deposit boxes inside.

The only customer the teller line had—an old woman with puffy white hair using a cane—finished her transaction and turned away and started toward the door.

The bank manager paused his conversation with the old man to say, "Have a great day, Audrey."

Audrey paused long enough to raise a hand of acknowledgement before shuffling past Janine toward the door.

Janine switched the suitcase from her right hand to her left hand as she stepped back to hold open the door for the old woman.

Audrey smiled at her and said thank you before shuffling outside.

Janine let the door close and approached the teller line again.

The teller stationed behind the counter asked, "Can I help you?"

Janine said, "I'd like to access my safe deposit box."

"Sure," the teller said. She picked up a phone and dialed a number, and the phone on one of the desks rang. The woman typing at the computer paused, looked up at Janine and the teller, and answered the phone. The teller said, "She'd like to access her box and I can't leave the front right now."

The woman at the desk said she'd be there in a minute.

The teller smiled at Janine. "Georgina will be right with you."

Just then Georgina pushed away from her computer and stood and approached Janine, flattening the creases in her pantsuit.

"Good morning," she said. "You need to access your box?"

"That's right," Janine said. "Box forty-seven."

Georgina didn't even blink. She said, "No problem. Marisa, can I have the vault keys?"

Marisa already had a small ring of keys ready.

As Georgina took the keys, the bank manager asked the old man to wait and hurried over. He said to Georgina, "I can take this."

"It's okay," Georgina said. "I've got it."

"Lloyd's asking about CDs again, and I know you're more familiar with the current rates than I am."

Georgina snickered. "Aren't you supposed to be the manager?"

"Yes, and that's why I deal with big business loans. Can you help him out?"

"Sure," she said, handing him the keys. Then said to Janine, smiling, "Don't ask him about CDs and you'll be fine," and left them to head back over to the desks.

"I'm Simon," the bank manager said. "You said you wanted to access box forty-seven?"

"Yes."

"Follow me."

He led her into the vault and set the ring of keys on the counter inside the door as he pulled open a drawer. Inside were several files, all with numbered tabs. He pulled out the file marked 47. The only thing inside was a signature card. At the top was the name ASHLEY GILMORE and below was a grid to mark every time Ashley accessed the box. It had only been accessed once, two years ago.

"You have your ID?" Simon asked.

Janine turned to him, nodding, reaching for the ID in her pocket, but Simon wasn't watching her, instead the camera up in the corner.

He glanced at the ID when she showed it and said, "Perfect," and handed her a pen and said, "Please sign on the line."

Janine set the suitcase aside and signed on the line right beneath where Ashley Gilmore had signed two years ago. The signature didn't look perfect—Janine had only had an hour to practice it based on the signature from Ashley's ID—but it would do in a pinch if Simon didn't scrutinize it too closely.

The bank manager didn't. As he did with the ID, he glanced at the signature and then added the file back with the others and closed the drawer. "Have your key?"

She slid the key from her pocket, already scanning the wall of boxes. Number 47 was a large box, near the floor.

"May I?" Simon said, holding out his hand.

She gave him the key, and he took it and inserted it into one of the slots, inserted the bank's master key, turned both, and opened the panel.

Inside was a large metal box, a clasp on the front to work as a handle.

Simon used the clasp to slide the box out from the slot. "Whoa, this is heavy. Would you like me to carry it to the room?"

For a moment Janine said nothing, trying to process the words. Then she nodded, said yes, and Simon set the box on the counter and closed the panel and took back the bank master key and handed her the other key and then hefted the metal box again.

"Would you mind?" he asked, tilting his chin at the door.

She grabbed the suitcase and held the door open for him and then followed another tilt of his chin to another door against the wall. Which, as it turned out, was a private room, a desk built into the wall with a chair in front of it and nothing else. No windows. No cameras. Completely private.

Simon set the box down on the table. "I'll be waiting outside for when you're done," he said, and left her, closing the door behind him.

Janine moved at once. She set the suitcase on the desk beside the metal box and lifted the lid. Despite having already known what would be inside it, she still found herself gasping at the contents.

One and a half million dollars, most of it bundles of hundreds. They weren't new bills, either, but worn bills, the kind that wouldn't raise any eyebrows if they were passed around. Were some of the bills marked? Most definitely. They'd have to ask Charles for more information once this was all over, assuming, of course, Charles even had that information.

But the money wasn't all that was inside the metal box. Tucked in a corner, almost as an afterthought, was a flash drive. A flash drive that supposedly showed what went down between Sean Wescott and Agent Weber two years ago.

The suitcase was just large enough to fit all the money. Janine loaded the suitcase as quickly as she could since Logan and Samuel expected her to return in fifteen minutes. The flash drive she tucked into her jeans pocket, right next to Ashley Gilmore's ID.

Janine closed the suitcase and kept it on the desk as she opened the door.

Simon stood several yards away. He forced a smile. "Ready?"

She nodded.

When he picked up the metal box, he said, "Wow, as light as a feather."

He led her back into the vault, setting the box aside and taking her key to open 47 again. Sliding the box inside, closing the door, locking it once again, he turned to her holding out the box key, and there was something different about his eyes, something strange.

Glancing once more at the camera in the corner, he said, "Will there be anything else?"

Janine shook her head. "That's all for today, thanks."

His gaze slid down to the suitcase in her hand, the heavy suitcase that she was straining to hold upright. He nodded and said, his voice a whisper, "I see."

Janine didn't know what to say, so she said nothing else. She exited the vault and made a beeline toward the exit.

As she reached the glass doors leading outside, Simon shouted, "Ms. Gilmore!"

Janine paused. Glanced back over her shoulder at the bank manager.

He forced another smile, this one all teeth. "Thanks once again for your business. Have a great day."

Everyone was watching her now—the teller, the two people waiting on line, even Georgina at the desk had paused in her typing to glance over her monitor at Janine.

Janine nodded, said, "Thanks," and pushed through the door into the stark morning sunlight.

47

They had barely exited the bank's parking lot when Logan said, "Well?"

Janine patted the suitcase on the backseat beside her. "There was no laptop, but the money's all in there. I didn't have time to count it all, but it's definitely a shitload."

"The flash drive?"

She pulled it from her pocket, held it up for him to see.

"Jesus Christ," Logan said. "Part of me didn't even think it was possible the thing existed."

Samuel accelerated down the highway, his gaze flicking toward the rearview mirror every couple seconds. "Now what?"

"Now we head back to the motel," Logan said. He flipped open Janine's cell phone, began dialing a number.

Samuel said, "Who are you calling?"

"Charles."

Logan placed the phone to his ear and listened several seconds before he said, "We got it. No, there was no laptop, just the money and a flash drive. No, we haven't had a chance to see what's on the flash drive yet; we literally just got it two minutes ago. Yes, we're headed back to the motel now. Okay, see you there."

As Logan closed the phone, Samuel said, "He's meeting us?"

"He said he's already on the way. Will arrive in an hour or so."

"Shit," Samuel said.

They looked at him.

Logan said, "What's wrong?"

Samuel was watching the rearview mirror. "I think the bank manager's following us."

Janine twisted in her seat to look out the back window. Sure enough, the black Honda Civic was tailing them several car lengths back.

"What should I do?" Samuel said.

Nobody answered him at first.

Janine said, "Pull over."

"*What?*"

"Not along here. Try to find somewhere private."

A quarter mile later they turned off into the parking lot of a strip mall. The Honda Civic pulled in right after them.

Samuel steered them around behind the buildings where only dumpsters and a few employee cars were parked. He stopped the sedan.

"Now what?"

Again nobody answered him. They waited and watched as the Honda Civic pulled up behind them and the bank manager stepped out, his hands in his coat pockets, his face red as he stalked toward them.

"Keep the engine running," Logan said, taking his Glock and stepping out of the sedan. He didn't move toward the bank manager, though, just stood there with the passenger door open, the gun held at his side out of the bank manager's line of sight. "Help you with something?"

"You're goddamned right you can help me with something." The bank manager nearly spat the words. "I want my fucking cut."

"Your cut?"

"Don't play games with me." He paused, studying Logan's

face. "You're the other one, aren't you? I thought they caught you again."

Logan glanced up and down the back of the strip mall, saw that they were still alone. "I'm afraid I don't know what you're talking about."

The bank manager brandished a small handgun from his coat pocket. He didn't aim it at Logan, but held it down at his side as if the presence of the gun alone should be enough to get his point across.

"Don't bullshit me," the bank manager said. "I did what I was told. They offered me a promotion to corporate, but I turned them down to stay at that shitty branch and keep an eye on the money and make sure the bitch didn't try to access it."

The bank manager's teeth were clenched, his chest rising and falling, working himself up.

"Shit, that's not even her. I don't know what the fuck's going on, but I knew Mr. Wescott would be coming for the money once I learned he'd escaped. Why else do you think I was working today?"

Logan said nothing at first. He dipped his head to look into the sedan, at Samuel and Janine, and then leaned back out to focus on the bank manager.

"How much are you owed?"

The bank manager licked his chapped lips. "Two hundred."

Logan smiled, shook his head. "I don't think so."

"Fine. It was one fifty." He shrugged, forced a complicit smile. "Can't blame a guy for trying, can you?"

"One hundred."

The smile faded. "What?"

"One hundred grand."

"No fucking way. The deal was one fifty."

"Yeah, but that was before you got greedy. Or do you want me to call Mr. Wescott and let him know what you tried to pull?"

At once fear flickered in the bank manager's eyes. "No, no.

I'm sorry. One hundred grand"—he swallowed—"one hundred is fine."

"Give me a moment," Logan said, and dipped his head back down into the sedan.

Janine said, "You aren't seriously going to give him any money, are you?"

Logan watched the bank manager through the sedan's rear window. "It's not a big deal. We give him the money now, pick him up later."

It was clear Samuel and Janine didn't think it was a good idea, but neither disputed this.

Janine turned in her seat, opened the suitcase, and began pulling out bundles of cash.

Logan leaned back out, asked the bank manager, "You got a bag?"

At first the bank manager looked confused. Then he nodded, drifting back to the Honda Civic. He kept the gun in his hand while he leaned into the car. Several seconds later he leaned back out, a plastic grocery bag in hand.

"Here," he said, extending it toward Logan but not walking any closer.

Logan approached, and for the first time the bank manager saw the Glock at Logan's side. His eyes widened slightly, his nostrils flared.

"What," Logan said, "you didn't think you were the only one packing, did you?"

The bank manager said nothing.

Logan took the bag from him, looked inside. "There's trash in here."

"Yeah, I use it for trash in my car. Look, it's the only bag I've got."

Inside the bag were crumpled napkins and tissues, a smashed McDonald's wrapper, and discarded French fries.

Logan handed the bag inside the car and waited while Janine

loaded it with enough bundles to make one hundred grand. This filled the bag considerably, and Logan tossed it to the bank manager.

"Nice doing business with you."

"Wait," the bank manager said. "I need to count it first."

"It's all there."

"I need to count it."

"You've got one minute."

At first the bank manager looked like he was going to argue the point, but then he stuffed the handgun in his pocket and tore open the bag and started sorting through the bundles. He didn't have time to count each bundle individually, but did thumb through the bundles to make sure each pack contained the same bill amount.

Finally he nodded, his focus once again on Logan. "Where is Mr. Wescott, anyway?"

"He's waiting for us," Logan said. "Probably won't be happy to hear you've delayed the delivery of his money."

The bank manager swallowed again. He said nothing else, only lowered himself back into the Civic. Conducted a hurried three-point turn and accelerated away.

As Logan got back into the sedan, Janine said, "You make for a half-decent thug."

Logan clicked in his seat belt, leaned his head back on the headrest. "What do you expect? For two years I was a criminal."

48

Logan entered the motel room first.

He went in with his weapon raised, checking first the bathroom, then the rest of the sparse area, before announcing the room was clear.

Janine and Samuel entered, Samuel lugging the suitcase, Janine with Samuel's laptop bag slung over her shoulder.

Samuel set the suitcase on one of the beds. He took a moment to straighten the suitcase so its corners were perpendicular to the edges of the bed, and then he stepped back, staring at it.

"Now what?" he asked.

"Now we wait," Logan said, crossing the room to the window overlooking the parking lot. He shifted the curtain, peeked outside.

Janine said, "Any sign of Charles?"

Logan let the curtain drop back in place. "Not yet."

Samuel said, "Should we count it?"

Janine smiled. "If you want to, go ahead."

Samuel kept staring at the suitcase. He licked his lips. "I just

... I've never seen so much money before. I mean, I've seen it in movies and on TV, but not in real life."

Logan crossed over to the bed, unsnapped the clasps, and raised the lid. "Feast your eyes."

Samuel's mouth dropped open at the sight of all the cash.

Janine had set Samuel's bag on the floor. Now she pulled out his laptop, set it on the desk in the corner.

She turned to Logan, holding up the flash drive. "Ready?"

He hesitated. "Honestly? No."

"We have to."

"I know. It's just ..." He shook his head. "Gloria was a good friend. So was David. I don't want to believe they were capable of doing ... what they supposedly did."

"Look," Janine said, "we don't even know what's on this flash drive. It could be porn. But I think we owe it to ourselves to look, to be one hundred percent sure. I mean, Christ, how are we supposed to explain what's happened? People died because of this operation."

None of them disputed her.

Janine turned back to the desk. She sat down and opened the laptop's lid, powered it on. A screen came up asking for a login and password.

"Samuel, do you mind?"

He stepped up beside her, typed in his password.

The desktop now accessible, Janine uncapped the flash drive and went to insert it into the port on the side of the laptop.

"Wait," Samuel said, grabbing her hand to hold it in place.

She looked up at him. "What's wrong?"

"We have no idea what's on there. Logan said Sean Wescott claimed it was a video, so that's what we've all been assuming it is, but what if it's, I don't know, a virus or something?"

"Isn't there a way you can figure that out?"

Samuel bit his lip, considering it. "Yeah, I think I can. Mind if I take your seat?"

Janine switched places with him, Samuel leaning forward in the chair, his fingers dancing over the keys as he brought up one program after another.

Logan drifted back over to the window overlooking the parking lot. Shifted the curtain to peek outside. Still no sign of Charles.

"Okay," Samuel said. He picked up the flash drive, waited a beat, and inserted it into one of the laptop's two side ports.

On the screen, one of his programs analyzed the flash drive's contents. It took ten seconds, and then Samuel said, "It appears clean."

Janine said, "What's on it?"

"Looks to be only one file. A video."

"Play it."

Samuel double-clicked the file. It took a moment to load, and then they had a grainy view of the inside of an abandoned building.

That was it. Nothing happened.

"Is it playing?" Janine asked.

"It is. Just nothing's going on."

Logan asked from his spot by the window, "How long does it run?"

"Looks to be three hours."

"Fast-forward it," Janine said.

Samuel accelerated the video's speed. An hour in, a car appeared and Samuel slowed the video to regular speed.

Agent David Weber stepped out of the car. He glanced around the building, leaned back against the car, his arms folded, waiting.

Fifteen minutes later another car arrived. Sean Wescott. He stepped out and shook Weber's hand, Sean making a surreptitious glance at the camera as if to confirm it was still there. The two chatted briefly, their voices muffled on the video. Still, it was clear when Agent Weber directed Sean Wescott to the back of the sedan and popped the trunk and showed him the duffel bag of cash inside. Sean Wescott whistled, nodding that he was impressed.

By that point Logan had drifted over to the desk, Janine standing on one side of Samuel, Logan on the other.

They watched as Sean Wescott chatted some more with Agent Weber. Agent Weber motioned for Sean to take the duffel bag. As Sean turned to grab the bag, Weber pulled out a gun. Sean, maybe sensing danger, turned in time to see the barrel leveling on him. He knocked the gun away, pulled out his own gun, and fired a round into Weber's stomach.

Agent Weber went down. Sean kept the gun aimed for another second before he lowered it. He crouched down, stood back up, crouched down again, clearly not sure what to do next. In the end, he grabbed the duffel bag from the sedan's trunk, hustled it over to his own car, threw it in the trunk, and got out of there.

"Son of a bitch," Logan murmured. "The bastard was telling the truth."

"We don't know that," Janine said. "Gloria hasn't shown up yet."

They didn't have to wait long. Less than ten minutes passed—all of them watching David Weber sit on the ground, his hand on his stomach, dying—before another car arrived. Agent Gloria Ramirez stepped out. She hurried over to Weber, asked him what happened. It didn't appear as if Weber could respond verbally, but he did nod and shake his head. Gloria stood back up, got out her phone, and dialed a number. Spoke a few words, put the phone away, and then just stood there, her back to Weber.

"My God," Janine said. "He's still alive."

Yes, but not for much longer. His arm had been moving in slow jerks, trying to get Gloria's attention, before it stopped moving completely.

Logan returned to his spot by the window. Peeked back out

at the parking lot. A sedan had pulled in. Charles climbed out, scanned the rooms, and started in their direction.

"Charles is here," Logan said.

Samuel said, "Maybe we should stop this for now."

Janine said, "No, let it play. How much more time is left?"

"Looks to be another hour."

"Fast-forward it again."

"I'm going to turn it off."

Janine leaned forward, hit the button to speed up the video. Gloria didn't move from her spot until eleven minutes later when another car appeared.

There was a soft knock at the motel room door.

Janine slowed the video's speed back to normal. She squinted at the laptop screen as a man stepped out of the new car.

Behind her, Logan started to open the motel room door.

Recognizing the new man in the video, Janine turned and shouted, "Don't!"

But it was already too late.

Logan had opened the door, his focus on Charles's face, his gaze only skipping down a half second later to the gun in Charles's grip, a sound suppressor screwed to its barrel.

49

Charles shoved the extended barrel into Logan's stomach, shot him once, Logan jerking as the bullet entered his body, and Charles pushed him backward as he entered the motel room, swinging the door closed behind him, raising the pistol toward Janine and Samuel in the corner by the desk.

Logan stumbled back, tripped over his own feet, and hit the carpet with a thud, both hands to the wound in his stomach.

Janine sprang for the closest bed, the one on which her holstered pistol lay, but before she could move a step, Samuel grabbed her arm and jerked her back, rising from the chair, a gun suddenly in his hand, its snub-nosed barrel pressed into the small of her back.

"Don't," he said.

Panicked, she looked from Samuel to Charles, from Charles to Samuel, to Logan writhing on the floor.

Charles stepped over Logan, keeping his weapon aimed at Janine. His gaze shifted to the laptop on the desk.

"I see the cat's out of the bag," he said. "I'm hoping only you three have seen it so far."

"Yes," Samuel said. "I tried to make them wait, but Janine refused."

Charles grinned at this. "Yes, Agent Snyder has always been a tad incorrigible."

Janine said, her voice filled with fury, "Why?"

"*Why?*" Charles grinned again, chuckling. "Not to be so blunt, but money, of course. One and a half million dollars. Me, Gloria, David—we'd worked it out perfectly. Set up a sting, use the money, but make it seem like Wescott took off with it."

Logan kept writhing on the floor. One hand still on his stomach, as if trying to hold in all the blood, his other hand reaching for his pocket.

"Gloria was waiting less than a mile away from the warehouse," Charles said. "She was going to help dispose of Wescott's body. Of course, none of us knew Wescott had recorded the entire thing. That definitely fucked over our plan. He'd called and spoke to Gloria briefly, told her what he'd done. She didn't believe him, of course, but then he told her exactly what he'd seen, both her and me, and, well, we knew that was a problem. Hell, it was his protection in a way. He said that if anything happened to him, the video would see the light of day. Couldn't quite take him out in prison, could we? That's why Gloria had to talk someone into meeting up with him inside. Someone who could, you know, break Wescott out."

Charles grinned at Logan.

"You did fine work, Agent Taylor. You should be proud of yourself."

Janine said, "Maryann?"

"She was a loose end. Her body wasn't supposed to be found for days, except it seems Warden Barnes got nosy."

"And Samuel?"

"He's one of my protégés. I put him on this operation to keep an eye on everything to make sure nobody fucked up. Hell, how do you think everybody got deleted from the database?"

"It wouldn't be hard to have us reinstated," she said.

"Of course," Charles said. "But that was before you decided to help Neal Palmer escape. After all, it will soon be known that he was taken into FBI custody. Then after that thing at the church—to be honest, I'm still trying to come up with a plausible explanation for that, but everyone is going to want to know what happened to Neal Palmer. It will turn out Janine helped him escape. Why? Who knows. Sometimes you never need a reason for things for the media to go apeshit. They'll love it. And so myself and Samuel managed to track you both here to this motel room. We tried to arrest you, but you both fought back and, well, I think you know how the story ends."

On the floor, Logan's trembling hand had managed to slip into his pants pocket. Now it came back out, gripping the switchblade.

Janine tilted her head, said to Samuel, "The least you can do is not shoot me in the back."

Samuel glanced toward Charles, who nodded his agreement. Samuel stepped away from Janine, pointing his pistol now at her head.

"Better?" he said.

Janine, who now had view of the entire room, said, "Much better."

At that same instant, the blade popped up from the knife in Logan's hand, a quiet *snick*.

Samuel noticed the sound, glanced away from Janine toward Charles.

Charles, who hadn't heard the sound, met Samuel's gaze. "What?"

Logan used all his strength to swing his arm back and plunge the blade into Charles's calf muscle.

Charles cried out, the extended barrel shifting away from Janine, his finger squeezing the trigger slightly, enough to release a round which struck the ceiling.

Janine threw all her weight at Samuel. She spun and drove her fist into his throat, wrestled the gun from his grip, and then shot him twice in the chest before spinning back toward Charles and firing two rounds into his chest.

Charles stumbled back to one of the beds. His own pistol fell from his grasp. He lay on the bed and did not get back up.

Janine double-checked that both men were dead, then scrambled over to Logan, who once again had both hands on his stomach.

His lips moved, producing no sound. He paused, licked his lips, tried again.

"The bullet ... is still ... in there."

She jumped to her feet, crashed into the bathroom, came back out with one of the towels. She balled the towel and pressed it against his stomach.

"Just ... go," Logan said.

"No"—she shook her head, keeping pressure on the wound— "I'm not leaving you."

"Take ... the money."

"*No*. It'll be okay. We can explain this."

His head moved from side to side, his eyes closing. "No ... we can't."

Janine was quiet for a moment, thinking. "I can get the bullet out. You'll be okay."

Logan didn't even bother telling her no. His head moved from side to side again.

"I won't let you die. I won't"—looking around the room frantically—"I need to get supplies. Then I'll take the bullet out. I'll get you patched up."

Logan stared up at her. His hand found hers. He squeezed.

"Go," he whispered. "Just ... go."

50

"Dorothy? Dorothy, come see this!"

Dorothy Sellers—sixty-five years old, a retired elementary teacher—sat at the kitchen table, one of her many Sudoku workbooks open before her, a pencil in her hand. Not looking up from the workbook, she said, "What is it, Harold?"

"They just released a new video. It's"—he paused, no doubt searching for the word—"*stunning*."

Dorothy made no move to get up from the table. "I'm sure it is, dear."

"Seriously, this changes everything."

She could hear the TV from the other room, Harold in his recliner, his feet up on the ottoman, one cable news channel or another running nonstop. After a minute she heard him sigh and push himself out of the recliner and shuffle into the kitchen.

"You missed it," he said.

Her focus still on the workbook, she said, "I'm sure they'll play it again."

"I'm sure they will too, but the video is pretty damning to the FBI."

She glanced up at him. "Are you ready for lunch yet?"

"I'm not hungry."

"How about I make us both some egg salad sandwiches?"

His nose wrinkled at the suggestion. "Now I'm definitely not hungry."

She grabbed the cane leaning against the table and rose from her chair, started toward the refrigerator.

Harold said, "A video was sent to the media. They say it shows Sean Wescott and that FBI agent, but Sean Wescott doesn't kill the agent. Or, well, I guess he does kill the agent, but it's because the agent tried to attack him, so Sean Wescott shot him first, and then—Are you listening?"

"Yes, dear," she said, taking the Saran-wrapped bowl from the fridge.

"They say on the video two other FBI agents show up after the fact. One of them was one of the agents who died in that church in Pennsylvania, another was one of the agents they found in that motel room. But, well, he wasn't even an agent. He was an assistant deputy director!"

Dorothy was at the counter now, taking two slices of wheat bread from the breadbox and laying them on a paper towel. She stepped over to the sink, turned on the water to wash her hands, but something caught her attention out through the window.

"Somebody's outside," she said.

"What's that?"

"A woman's outside."

Harold shuffled forward, squinted through the window overlooking the driveway. Sure enough, a woman was out there, circling the boat propped up on the trailer.

"Looks like we've got ourselves a prospective buyer," Harold said.

"If she's a serious buyer, don't mess it up."

Harold was already heading over to the closet to grab his jacket. "What do you mean?"

"The price, Harold. I told you it was way too high. That's why the boat's been sitting in our driveway for the past six months. Quote her something reasonable. I'd love for it to be gone before Christmas."

He smiled at her, zipping up his jacket. "I'll see what I can do."

The young woman outside looked up as he stepped out of the house. "Afternoon," he said.

She smiled at him. "Sorry if it seems like I was snooping. I wanted to take a look first before I knocked at your door."

"No problem at all."

"How long have you had this?"

"Oh, it's been over a decade now. My wife and I bought it new when it first came out. We'd take it down to the bay and steer it out into the ocean. Kept it down at the docks for a while, but the fees became too ridiculous. Then again, with its size, it's pretty ridiculous to keep it here in the driveway."

He chuckled, took a breath to start his pitch.

"Do you know much about boats? This is a 2004 Stingray 240 CS. It's a cabin cruiser, twenty-four feet long, and, well, did you want to take a look inside?"

The woman stood motionless for a moment, studying the boat. Then she turned to Harold and asked, "How much?"

"I'm sorry?"

"What are you asking for it?"

Harold hesitated. "Forty grand, and that includes the trailer."

She offered him a thin smile. "Realistically this boat probably isn't worth more than thirty."

At first Harold said nothing, just stared at the woman. He chuckled again. "Okay, you got me. Maybe I am overpricing it. But that's the fun of it, right? We get to negotiate." He grinned. "Sorry, I used to be a car salesman."

The woman said, "Thirty even."

Harold frowned, biting his lower lip. He glanced back at the house, at Dorothy watching them through the kitchen window, then turned back to the woman.

"I think we can make that work. We're just gonna have to find a notary to—"

"No," the woman said. "No notary. Simple swap."

Harold's frown deepened. He studied the woman's face again. "What's the hurry?"

"No hurry. It's just my husband and I can't wait to go boating."

"It's the first week of December. Too cold to boat."

"Here in South Carolina maybe. But we're thinking about heading south."

Had Harold taken a moment to look, he would have seen there was no ring on the woman's finger. Instead he glanced up the driveway for the first time at the SUV parked by the mailbox. A man sat in the passenger seat. The man had his head back on the headrest, sunglasses on his face.

As if sensing Harold watching him, Logan Taylor tilted his head toward the old man and raised a hand, his other hand resting on his wrapped and healing stomach.

Harold returned the wave, then said to the woman, "Okay, I think we can make thirty grand work. Not a personal check, though. Only a cashier's check."

Janine Snyder smiled. "How about cash?"

ABOUT THE AUTHOR

Robert Swartwood is the *USA Today* bestselling author of *The Serial Killer's Wife*, *The Calling*, *Man of Wax*, and several other novels. He created the term "hint fiction" and is the editor of *Hint Fiction: An Anthology of Stories in 25 Words or Fewer.* He lives with his wife in Pennsylvania.

Printed in Great Britain
by Amazon